Matthew Blagden Hale

The Aborigines of Australia

being an account of the institution for their education at Poonindie, in

South Australia, founded in 1850

Matthew Blagden Hale

The Aborigines of Australia
being an account of the institution for their education at Poonindie, in South Australia, founded in 1850

ISBN/EAN: 9783337313852

Printed in Europe, USA, Canada, Australia, Japan

Cover: Foto ©Andreas Hilbeck / pixelio.de

More available books at **www.hansebooks.com**

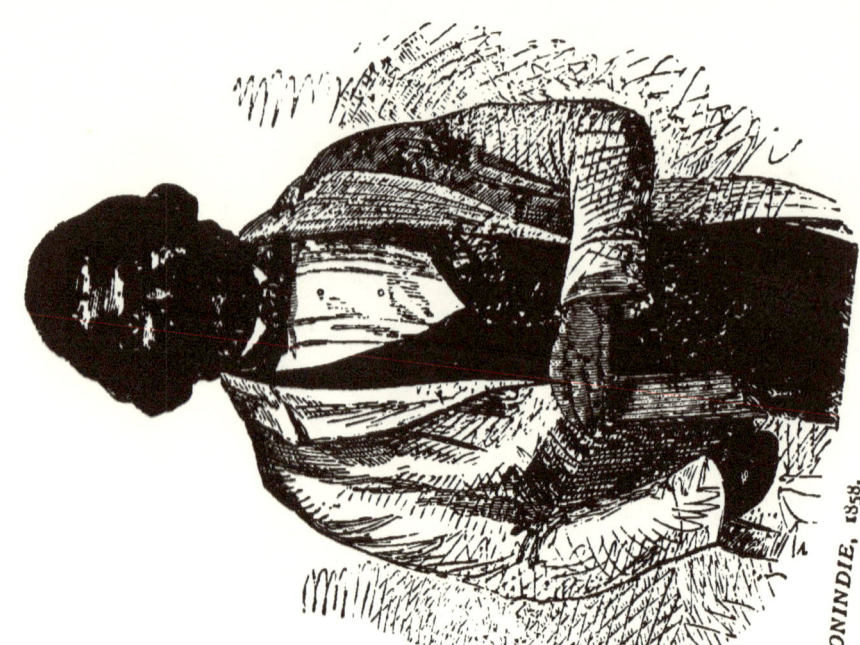

NATIVES EDUCATED AT POONINDIE, 1858.

THE

ABORIGINES OF AUSTRALIA,

BEING AN ACCOUNT OF

THE INSTITUTION FOR THEIR EDUCATION

AT

POONINDIE,

IN SOUTH AUSTRALIA.

Founded in 1850 by the Ven. ARCHDEACON HALE, a Missionary of S.P.G.

BY THE

RIGHT REV. BISHOP HALE.

PUBLISHED UNDER THE DIRECTION OF THE TRACT COMMITTEE.

LONDON:
SOCIETY FOR PROMOTING CHRISTIAN KNOWLEDGE,
NORTHUMBERLAND AVENUE, CHARING CROSS, W.C.;
43, QUEEN VICTORIA STREET, E.C.
BRIGHTON: 135, NORTH STREET.
NEW YORK: E. & J. B. YOUNG & CO.

THE ABORIGINES OF AUSTRALIA.

I PROPOSE in the following pages to give some account of the first formation of the Natives Institution of Poonindie in South Australia. It was established in the year 1850 for training and Christianizing some members of the aboriginal race, and it is now (in 1889) still carrying on its beneficent work.

But it seems right that I should, in the first instance, explain how it came about that I, having gone to Australia in the same ship with the Bishop of Adelaide when he first went out, to be his Archdeacon, should after-wards have devoted myself specially to work amongst the natives, allowing the work properly pertaining to me as Archdeacon to fall almost into abeyance.

My explanation must carry me back to the time of the emancipation of the slaves in the West Indies. At that time I thought much and deeply upon the great responsi-bility which rested upon us, as a nation, with reference to those heathen races, which, in various parts of the world, had become subject to British rule. As regards the slaves just alluded to, I had very great doubts whether the measures which were being adopted for the amelioration of their condition would be really beneficial to them if those measures should be terminated by the mere Act of Emancipation.

It appeared to me that the slaves, when freed from the compulsory control of those who had been their masters, would be subject to no control at all, unless some powerful moral influence could be brought to bear upon them, in place of the physical restraint from which they were being relieved, and I know of no moral influence which could be

B

brought to bear upon them except by means of Christian teaching.

So strong was this feeling within me that, before I was ordained, I earnestly desired to go to the West Indies and to devote myself to the work which appeared to me to be so loudly called for. Acting upon this desire I went to the office of S.P.G. I was probably unfortunate in the clergyman with whom I had an interview. My visit was not encouraging, and I did not repeat it. Subsequently, in a well considered letter to my father, I made a definite proposition to go to the West Indies. But the proposition was received so unfavourably by all the members of my family that I gave up the project, and eventually I entered upon a curacy in this country.

But the feeling, which had impelled me to take the steps just described, never left my mind. I frequently spoke at meetings, of S.P.G., and also for C.M.S.; and, from time to time, I said to myself, " It is one thing to stand on " a platform and to hold forth about the duty of going to " the heathen; but it is quite another thing to go oneself." However, during the first eleven years that I was in Holy Orders, my own path of duty seemed plain enough. It seemed clear to me, during those years, that my work was in the mother country.

Then came the year 1847, when four Bishops, all for the Colonies, were consecrated in Westminster Abbey, on St. Peter's Day. It was a great day for the Colonial Church, and I do not hesitate to say that, in consequence of the impetus which was then given to the cause of missionary work generally, it was a great day for the Church at home.

A few weeks after this event I was staying in the house with one of those Bishops—Dr. Short, the Bishop for Adelaide, South Australia—and I had many conversations about the Church in the Colonies, and about the treatment of the aboriginal inhabitants; and one day, during one of our conversations (we were walking), the Bishop, in that peculiar abrupt way, which every one who knew the dear old man will remember, stopped, and facing about, and standing opposite to me said, in his peculiar, short, quick manner, " You must come out, and be my " Archdeacon." The thought of going out with him had never entered my mind; but, when I came seriously to consider the matter, I could see that there really was no good and sufficient reason why I should not obey the call which seemed to be thus sent to me.

For nearly six years I had borne the weight of the duties of the parish of Stroud—a parish of 8,000 inhabitants, to which I had been appointed by Bishop Monk. But in 1845 I was compelled, by the effect upon my mind of a great sorrow, to resign it. In 1847 I, and my two little motherless children, were living with my father, who had also not long become a widower, in Wiltshire. I had taken charge of a small country parish, a daughter parish of Bradford-on-Avon, and connected with my father's property. One of my brothers (unmarried) was, at the time I met Bishop Short, returning with his regiment from India, and I knew that he could take my place with my father. Circumstanced as I was, my arrangements were speedily made ; and, on the 2nd of September, I and my children and two female servants embarked in the same ship with the Bishop and his family and two other clergymen, whom he had engaged for work in his new diocese.

During the early part of the voyage I kept a diary, in the hope that some opportunity might occur by which I might send it back to England for the information of my friends. I must here give an extract from it, explaining that on the day on which this was written, the Bishop was preparing a document for my formal appointment of Archdeacon on our arrival in Adelaide. And he had been good enough to call me into his cabin to be present as assessor while he was so engaged. My remark written afterwards was as follows :—
" The puzzling out of a beginning of things in a new
" diocese will be a peculiar and difficult kind of work.
" But it has its charms for my mind, and I much hope and
" pray for grace and guidance to get pretty well through it.
" Being thrown so much together, I have, of course, seen a
" great deal of the Bishop, and have become very intimate
" with him ; and the more I see of him, the more thankful
" I am that, having been so long desirous of entering upon
" such an enterprise as the present one, I have been led to
" embark in this one with such a man as the Bishop of
" Adelaide." Written Feb. 24th, when we had been about three weeks at sea.

These little personal explanations have seemed to me

to be necessary in order that the reader may understand that there had been in my mind, for a considerable time, a readiness (if I may so express it) to enter upon work such as that which I am about to describe.

On our arrival in Adelaide we found that the Government had not been altogether unmindful of their duty to the aborigines. Very excellent schools for native children of both sexes had been for some time in existence in close proximity to Government House. The children were lodged and boarded on the school premises; but there were frequently absentees. The adult natives, hanging about the town, would often get some of them away for days, and even for weeks, together. Those, however, who attended with any degree of regularity, made fair progress with their lessons, and proved that they were quite capable of receiving instruction, and, with God's blessing, of receiving into their minds the first seeds of Christian truth.

But we learned, with sorrow, that there was no arrangement in existence by means of which these young people, so long and often successfully cared for, could be guided and protected after they had outgrown the school. Just at the ages when they most needed care and guidance they were thrown upon their own resources, and lost to civilization. Hence the need of some supplemental institution into which they might be received at this critical period of their lives.

It will, I presume, be clearly understood that nothing could be done towards carrying out any such scheme as seemed to be required without the sanction and assistance of the Government. Happily, the gentleman who, at the time I am now speaking of, was Governor of South Australia was Sir Henry Edward Fox Young, and it gives me much pleasure to record here how thoroughly and heartily he entered into the scheme, and how ready he was to assist me in every way. In fact it would have been quite impossible for me to have attempted to carry out my project if Sir Henry Young had been apathetic or half-hearted about it.

As my narrative will show, important concessions from the Government were absolutely necessary in order that the scheme might be put upon a proper footing. And I never should have obtained those concessions if the

Governor had not used his influence on my behalf with the other members of the Executive.

The necessity for the thing having been acknowledged, I, at first, appeared simply in the character of the person deputed to put some definite plan before His Excellency on paper. I had two or three interviews with him concerning the said scheme, and made certain alterations which he suggested. Finally the thing was brought into such a shape as to meet with his full approval. Then he said, "And, now, who is to do it?" And he evidently had not at all expected the answer which I made when I replied that, with His Excellency's permission, I was prepared to undertake it. The Bishop's permission was, of course, also necessary. But I knew that that would be given.

I now introduce a letter written to the Governor by myself, and His Excellency's reply. These documents led to the immediate commencement of work. In this letter the name of Mr. Moorhouse is mentioned. It will be frequently mentioned in the course of the narrative. He was a Government officer, the Protector of Aborigines. The children, while in Adelaide, were in his charge. He also fell in with the scheme thoroughly and heartily, and was always ready to take any amount of trouble to help me.

FROM ARCHDEACON HALE TO HIS EXCELLENCY SIR
EDWARD HENRY FOX YOUNG.

August 17th, 1850.

" MAY IT PLEASE YOUR EXCELLENCY,

"I am encouraged, by the observations which fell from your Excellency this morning, to address you again on the subject of the contemplated Natives Institution.

" The despatches which have reached your Excellency by the *Candahar* appear to leave no doubt upon your mind as to the answer which will be returned to your Excellency's despatch of the 12th of July last. And I further gather from your observations that, under the influence of this feeling, you would be willing to sanction the opening of the Institution, *on a modified scale*, without further delay.

" That there should be as little delay as possible before commencing operations is, in my opinion, a matter of great importance. The great need for the establishment of such an institution arises from the necessity of so extending the means which are at present in use for the benefit of the natives that they may not be thrown back wholly upon their own resources when they leaye the school.

" It appears that there are now at the present time 'a set' of school children of both sexes just arriving at this critical age. Mr. Moorhouse has many times described their state to me by saying 'they are just now ' fit to be put under a missionary's care.' They have got all that they will get from the school. They can, for the most part, read and write and cast accounts, and are acquainted with the leading principles and facts of the Christian religion.

" If these young people are left to go their own way for the next eight or ten months, there is every reason to suppose (because the same thing has happened over and over again with their predecessors) that they will by that time have become vitiated and corrupted, either by being drawn away again to their former wild habits of life or by associating with the dregs of the population of this city.

" So great is the anxiety of Mr. Moorhouse to preserve them from these contaminating influences that he has already run the risk of sending four young couples to Port Lincoln, in order that they may be there ready to enter the institution whenever it shall be ready for their reception.

" On account of these persons I think it extremely important that no time should be lost in commencing operations. They will, for the present, be assigned as servants, to certain persons in and about Port Lincoln. But experience has too often proved that, however kind and well-disposed settlers may be towards the natives, they will not *take the pains* with them, nor exercise *that degree of vigilance* and care which is necessary to prevent their falling back from those good habits which they may have acquired at the school. Their instruction is, at any rate, quite certain to be neglected.

" But there exist even stronger reasons why they should

not be left in the position above described. For natives
of Port Lincoln to return overland from Adelaide to
that settlement has become a very common practice;
and, inasmuch as the Adelaide natives in question will
have frequent opportunities of seeing and conversing
with those who have already performed the overland
journey, there is great reason to apprehend that they
may be induced to attempt to return to their homes.

" Now any attempt of this kind, successful or unsuc-
cessful, would be extremely prejudicial to the prospects
of the contemplated institution, on account of the feeling
which it would give rise to amongst the Adelaide
natives.

" The original scheme might be modified in a very
easy and simple manner by merely leaving out, for the
present, the juvenile department. There are five couples
of our Adelaide natives already at Port Lincoln. Mr.
Moorhouse might take measures for pairing off a few more
couples of the young people now leaving the school ; and
our operations for the next few months might be confined
to these married couples.

" A grant of £200 and rations for a definite number of
such couples for twelve months (the number to be fixed by
your Excellency, after conference with Mr. Moorhouse)
would enable us at once to commence operations upon
this scale.

" It would be unjust to the Colonists to omit to mention
to your Excellency the many circumstances which have
occurred to encourage me to press forward in this enterprise. I beg, first and foremost, to state that there are
two persons, whom I believe to be most single-minded
and devoted in their purpose, who are willing to go to
work with me at any moment as coadjutors. Mr. Henry
Minchin, as schoolmaster, and Mr. John Martin, as
superintendent of out-door works. The latter person is,
I think, exactly the man for the situation—an experienced
labourer, fencer, and sawyer, of 45 years of age. They
both desire to devote themselves to the work from motives
of piety, and because they lament and mourn over the
miseries of the unhappy blacks.

" I would next state that I find that there exists a degree
of interest in this scheme amongst the quiet, retiring portion
of our Colonists, which is generally much underrated. I there-

fore anticipate considerable support from private sources, and, with the amount of assistance above specified from public funds, I have no doubt of being able to carry on matters to the satisfaction of the Government until your Excellency receives the answer to your despatch of July 12th.

" I remain, &c.,

" MATTHEW B. HALE."

NOTE, 1889.—The answer to the said despatch of July 12th, 1850, was not received in Adelaide until the end of November, 1851. This will show how extremely important it was to my undertaking to have to deal with a Governor like Sir Henry Young, who gave me his hearty support, and was not afraid to act upon his own responsibility when he saw that it was needful to do so. The Institution was fourteen months old when Sir Henry received the reply to his first request to the Home Government to be permitted to establish it :

" FROM SIR HENRY YOUNG TO ARCHDEACON HALE.

" 24th August, 1850.

" DEAR ARCHDEACON,

" I have the pleasure of informing you that the modified proposal contained in your letter of the 17th is approved. You will learn from Captain Sturt, or the Auditor-General, Mr. Singleton, the forms to be gone through for obtaining the Grant.

" Yours sincerely,

" H. E. F. YOUNG."

Having thus obtained the sanction of his Excellency the Governor, I was able to prepare for work without delay. My next step was to put forth a prospectus explaining, for the information of the colonists, what I proposed to do, and the principles of action by which I hoped to be guided in my proceedings. The said prospectus was put forth as a letter addressed to the Editor of *The South Australian Register.*

It was as follows :

9

PROSPECTUS

OF AN INSTITUTION ABOUT TO BE FORMED AT PORT LINCOLN
FOR THE RELIGIOUS INSTRUCTION AND MORAL
TRAINING OF ABORIGINAL NATIVES.

[From the *South Australian Register*, August 28th, 1850.]

To the Editors of the " South Australian Register."

" Gentlemen—I trust you will permit me, through your pages, to address a few words to your readers on a subject which cannot be otherwise than interesting to every Christian mind, and which ought not to be a matter of indifference to any inhabitant of this colony. That subject is the spiritual condition of the aboriginal natives. My object in calling attention to it is to make a statement with respect to an effort which is about to be made to ameliorate the condition of certain individuals of this unhappy race.

" Every one, who is acquainted with the measures which have of late years been in operation for the instruction of aboriginal children in the neighbourhood of this city, must have this conviction, that further means—over and above those at present in use—are required in order to accomplish anything permanently beneficial.

" The whole means at present employed consist of *schools* for the *children* of either sex. They are only schools—the machinery is not calculated or adapted to accomplish more than would be accomplished by schools in any other place under similar circumstances. The case is pretty much the same as that of Ragged Schools in any of the large cities of England : children are collected to receive instruction from dark alleys and filthy courts, from the daily companionship of relations and associates of the lowest grade of society. If no efficient measures were taken to separate the scholars from such associates—if no means were employed to give those scholars, if they should wish it, a reasonable opportunity of carrying out Christian practices in their daily life—who would expect any other result from the Ragged School than that the scholars therein taught should go forth from it, sharpened in intellect indeed, more apt for every deed of mischief; but still rogues, thieves, pickpockets, as their parents and associates had been before them.

" The point which I wish to illustrate must be sufficiently obvious. Every reflecting person must see that
something must be added to the schools, as at present con-
stituted, before we can entertain any hope of their being
permanently useful to the natives.

" Three distinct sets of children have now been instructed in that school since its foundation, and have gone
forth again upon the world. Their position, upon leaving
the school, becomes at once one of banishment from the
sound of the Gospel of Christ. Their habits are such as
to prevent the employment of any agency to keep them in
mind of that Supreme Being whose name they have been
taught to call upon. They are without pastoral superintendence, without the means of grace, without refuge or
protection from the contaminations of vice which surround
them on every side. The school has not been without
instances of youths who have given the plainest indications of being under strong religious impressions ; but what
youthful piety—unless indeed sustained by a miracle of
grace—could stand against the torrent of vice which must
assail the poor young native who goes forth amongst the
manifold temptations of this place.

" I now proceed to the statement which I wish to lay
before your readers, viz., that an attempt is about to be
made to supply the grand desideratum, in order to turn to
better account those means which are at present in use.
An institution is about to be formed, where those natives
who have been brought up at the Adelaide School, and
others who may seem fit subjects for admission into it,
may be gathered together in one little community apart
from the vicious portion of the white population and the
wild portion of the blacks, where they may be kept under
regular Christian instruction, and enjoy the means of
grace—where the attempt may be made to lead them by
degrees into habits of industry and a more settled mode of
life.

" And here, if space would permit, I should be tempted
to answer in anticipation the objections which will be
raised by some persons against any such scheme, on the
ground of its hopelessness, and the consequent *so-called*
waste of time, and trouble, and money which will be
incurred. I shall, however, content myself with one single
answer. It is unphilosophical in the highest degree, it is

unreasonable, it is bigoted, to condemn any proposed experiment as hopeless, because certain other experiments, bearing some degree of resemblance to it, have been tried without success. It is by trying again and again, correcting each later experiment by the information derived from former failures, that success in all difficult cases is ultimately to be obtained. That success in the case before us is *possible*, no one who believes the Scriptures can doubt ; being *men*, it cannot be *impossible* that these natives should come to the knowledge of the truth, and obtain eternal life. There may be certain extraneous circumstances acting upon them which may render them, humanly speaking, incapable, for the time being, of receiving Divine knowledge ; but to say that the individual men, women, and children, of any given race *are absolutely and essentially incapable* of attaining to everlasting life, would be a position which I trust no one would venture to advance. If, then, there is a way of guiding these benighted beings into the paths of eternal happiness, how shall we dare to stay our efforts, or say that we are weary of the work, until we shall have exhausted every means which God shall put it into our power to attempt ?

" Here, again, it would be well pleasing to me to enlarge upon the great motives to missionary exertion which should prompt the inhabitants of this colony to assist, to the utmost of their power, in carrying out this good work. We might many of us, with much advantage to ourselves, indulge in such reflections as these—that although we may have, in our own minds and in a very easy and summary manner, settled all questions relating to the occupation of this country by the right of conquest—these questions have hereafter to be tried again before a much higher and more impartial tribunal than any earthly judgment seat. The Anglo-Saxon race are deriving countless wealth from the sunny hills and dales of South Australia, we have acquired here a noble country, destined, perhaps, to sustain its millions of population in prosperity and power. Hereafter we shall have to give an account of the return which has been made to the original proprietors of this territory ? What have we bestowed upon them as a recompense for the wrongs, the privations, the miseries, which they have suffered through our intrusion ?

" But it is time that I should now confine myself to the

particulars of the scheme which is proposed at the present time. It has already been stated, in the heading of this paper, that Port Lincoln has been selected as the locality for the intended Institution. Our natives, from this part of the colony, will be there removed from the influences which the elders of their own tribes at present exercise over them; and it is known from experience that natives who have been brought up as strangers to each other are by no means forward to associate together in the wild state. There is therefore scarcely any reason to fear that our people will ever wish to forsake the Institution with a view to join the Port Lincoln natives in their bush life. It is hoped also that they may be prevented from making any attempt to return to this part of the colony overland: the fear which they have of the Port Lincoln natives on account of their wilder and more daring character will go far in deterring them from making this experiment. But our unwearied endeavour will be to engender in their minds a feeling of real attachment towards the Institution as their home; we shall give to the married couples their own hut, their own plot of ground, their regular, though light and easy daily employment, we shall contrive variety and change in their occupations, and add a due admixture of relaxation and amusement; and, above all, we shall strive to make them feel the value of a settled mode of life as affording them the means of religious instruction, and of enabling them to attend to those things which concern their everlasting welfare.

" With respect to the willingness of the young natives to go from Adelaide to Port Lincoln, this point has already been ascertained. Five young couples have actually gone to that settlement, where for the present they are cared for and employed by certain settlers in that district. There are several more still about Adelaide who are quite willing to follow the example thus set them.

" In the first instance these young married couples only will be admitted to the Institution. Schools for the children of either sex will next be added, so soon as our means and other opportunities enable us to adopt this measure.

" We next come to the question of the *support* of the Institution. It is to be carried on by means of funds conjointly furnished by the Colonial Government and by voluntary contributions, administered through the Church of England. The latter for her part will *find*, *pay*, and *support* the living agency, *i.e.*, the Missionary Superintendent, and all other Europeans employed in conducting the affairs of the Institution. I make bold to undertake for her that she will never do *less* than this. I shall hope and trust that she will do more. I more especially trust that she will do more at our first commencement ; that we may be enabled to make a good beginning, and have no *unnecessary* difficulties to contend with.

" The Government aid at present granted amounts to the sum of £200 for the erection of the necessary huts, and the promise to maintain a limited number of married couples for a period of twelve months. In the mean time, his Excellency the Governor is in correspondence with the Home Government on the subject ; and there can be scarcely the shadow of a doubt but that, if the scheme proves itself to be worthy of support, assistance will hereafter be given to a much larger extent. But while this increased assistance is as yet only in prospect, we trust that the measure will be cordially and liberally supported by the inhabitants of this colony. With £200 to expend upon the erection of huts, the purchase of tools, implements, the necessary articles of simple furniture, and the various other needful appliances, we *can* make a beginning, it is true, but what sort of a beginning it would be, I will leave each person to judge for himself. But, no ! I will not believe that the colonists of South Australia will permit that the first expenditure in such a cause should be limited to this sum.

" Our first care, however, must be to see our living agency provided for by means of voluntary contributions. The unworthy individual whose name is attached to this paper, has the honour of being appointed to the superintendence of this enterprise ; he asks nothing of the colonists for himself—but he does ask a provision for those true-hearted men who have pressed forward to join him in the work, who are ready to go to it without fee or reward ; and are determined, " having food and raiment, to be therewith content." But " the labourer is worthy of his hire ;" and, however well it may become them to set forward thus in this labour of love, it would ill-become us to permit them to remain unrequited as to worldly goods, and without that compensation to which they will be so justly entitled.

" These men are Mr. Henry Minchin, assistant religious instructor and schoolmaster ; and Mr. John Martin, assistant schoolmaster and superintendent of out-door works. One other person it will be highly advisable to add to the establishment, viz., some Christian-minded female, rather advanced in life, who would teach and superintend the female natives, and instruct them in the performance of their domestic duties. If we fail in finding either the person suited to this position, or the means of securing her services, it will be necessary to authorise one of the native women to perform these duties so far as she may be able to do so. I trust we may have it in our power to make an arrangement less unsatisfactory than this would be.

" One word more, gentlemen, and I bring this lengthy letter to an end. I have now only to entreat, to implore, that the prayers and intercessions of those who address themselves to the Throne of Grace may be earnestly offered up in behalf of myself and those who will be associated with me in this arduous undertaking. We desire to go forth to our work with a single eye to the glory of our common Saviour, striving, after His example, ' to seek and to save that which was lost.' To all our Christian-minded friends, who love such works of piety, we reiterate again and again—*pray for us* that this one work may prosper in our hands.

" I am, Gentlemen,

" Your obedient servant,

" MATTHEW B. HALE,

" Archdeacon of Adelaide.

" Adelaide, *August 26th*, 1850."

As soon as possible after this we proceeded with our work, and, a few months later, having been asked to give some account of our doings for publication in a little local periodical, I give the following extracts :—

" On the 10th September we set up our tent upon Boston Island—an island of great beauty and many attractions, forming the shelter to the far-famed harbour of Port Lincoln. It will readily be understood, from the remarks which I have made above, that our object in choosing that locality was principally *seclusion*—that we might be cut off from the society of blacks living in a wild state, and protected from the unwelcome intrusions of evil-minded persons amongst the whites. These advantages we set against the formidable disadvantage that no permanent fresh water had, as yet, been discovered upon the island. We thought that we should be in a position to make a closer search for this necessary element than had ever been made before —we trusted much to the acknowledged natural sagacity of the natives in such cases—we determined to persevere in making well after well, so long as a hope remained of our obtaining the object of our search. However, all our expectations—all our efforts proved fruitless. *Salt* water! *Salt* water! was the oft-told tale of every well that was sunk. So prevalent is salt in the composition of the soil, above as well as below, that even the rain-water as it trickles down the sides of the hills, when but newly fallen from the clouds, tastes almost like the briny sea itself. Our wants in the mean time had been mainly supplied from a fine natural reservoir in a rock, where pure water to the amount of about 150 gallons is deposited by every moderate shower of rain ; and which we duly and carefully stowed away in casks for our daily use. But the angry ocean deprived us of even this resource. High and secure as our reservoir appeared upon ordinary occasions, the foaming billows beat up into it, on the occurrence of a storm, and showed us that even this resource might at any time fail us in the hour of greatest need.

" I need scarcely add that after this we abandoned the island. But the beauty of its scenery—the romantic wildness of its hills—the state of seclusion in which we had lived, and the primitive habits of life to which we had conformed during our sojourn of one short month upon its shores, made us all feel some measure of attachment towards it ; and I believe scarcely one of our party, whether white or black, quitted it without some feelings of regret.

" We had been, of course, thrown entirely upon our own resources as to our habitations, and a round or bell tent, which was kindly lent to us by the Surveyor-General, served for a shelter for our stores and such other things as most required protection from the weather, as well as for a sleeping apartment for the females of our little party. With respect to ourselves, the men (both white and black), the particulars of our sleeping apartment are soon given : an

ample fire to counteract the keenness of the night air,—
some closely wattled branches to defend us from the wind,
and the glorious canopy of heaven for a roof over our heads
—thus did we pass the first nights of our residence upon
Boston Island.

" Our exertions by day were of course directed to the
formation of a hut. The materials which presented them.
selves were long gum poles of a kind which I do not
remember to have seen anywhere else in the colony—they
are of all lengths up to 16 or 17 feet, the longest being five or
six inches in diameter at the larger end. The character of
this material seemed plainy to indicate to us that our
intended habitation would be most conveniently erected
in the shape of a Λ hut. A small shrub, apparently a
species of broom, formed an excellent material for thatching
the same. Accordingly in due time, Mr. Rayner being the
director of the operations, a very commodious habitation
was the result of our labours ; the dimensions being 32 feet
in length by 12 in width. Having accomplished this object
in order to secure to ourselves some degree of comfort in
the event of unsettled weather, we next directed our
attention to an active and energetic search for permanent
fresh water—of the result of these labours I have already
informed you."

When I found, as above explained, that our position on
Boston Island, was absolutely untenable, I wrote another
letter to the Governor, explaining all the circumstances of
the case, and praying for the sanction of the Government
to our removal to the main land. After most careful
consideration, I had come to the conclusion that a
locality about ten miles, by land, from Port Lincoln, was,
I considered, admirably suited to our purpose. And the
following extracts from my letter will explain the nature
of the petition which I then made.

Our party at this period was composed of thirteen
persons—five native couples (one couple having joined
us on the island) Mr. Minchin, Mr. Raynor, and myself. Under what circumstances Mr. Rayner took the
place of Mr. John Martin, previously mentioned, I do not
at all remember. Mr. Rayner was quite an elderly man ;
but still strong and active, and handy at work of all
kinds ; but, unfortunately, he had a temper, and he did

not remain with us long. The following are the extracts referred to :—

" The Tod opens into South Bay in Spencer's Gulf about nine miles by sea, from Port Lincoln. There are on and about it thirty-five sections of surveyed land. These sections cannot be said to be in much request amongst settlers, inasmuch as, although they have been surveyed and laid out for eight years, only two of them have ever been purchased. The proprietor of one lives in England, and the other in Adelaide. Neither of them have ever derived a fraction of profit from the sections. My petition, therefore, to your Excellency is that the remaining thirty-three sections be declared Natives Reserves (three of them, by the way, are Native Reserves already, and means will be taken to re-purchase the two already sold), that they be let to some responsible body (say the Society for the Propagation of the Gospel in Foreign Parts), for the purposes of the Institution ; upon the longest lease possible at a *nominal* rent, so long as the Institution should continue in a vigorous and efficient state. But if the native inmates of the Institution should, at any time, be so reduced in number (the exact minimum number should be specified) as to afford sufficient evidence that the scheme was not succeeding, it should then be competent for the Colonial Government to demand a *real* rent for or call upon, the parties connected with the Institution to give up the bulk of the sections, retaining at the *nominal* rent a number of sections only proportionate to the number of inmates still connected with the Institution, at the rate of one section for every adult native and one section for every two children.

" I need say nothing in support of the practice of making Native Reserves, nor of granting a section for the benefit of one individual native (as in the case of a black woman marrying a white man), since these practices have already received the sanction of precedent and of the highest authorities. I will only say that there is every probability that the number of inmates in our Institution will be sufficient to entitle them to ask for these sections upon the plea that they wish to settle upon them, and how infinitely greater will be the probability of their deriving benefit from them, granted in this way, than if they were granted as isolated sections, scattered throughout the Colony.

c

" I now proceed to explain how I propose to use this land for the benefit of the natives. It forms no part of my scheme to make them *settlers* on their own account in the *early stage* of their training. I would work a small farm on account of the general fund of the concern, and employ the individual natives as labourers at fixed wages.

" I must here explain that it is intended even from the first, to give every man his own separate hut, with his little garden, to be cultivated at leisure times."

My letter then goes on to explain the absolute necessity for having not only the surveyed sections under the control of the Institution, but also the small sheep run surrounding those sections. I remark that, so long as the run is in the hands of any person not associated with us in our undertaking, we should be liable to the intrusion of shepherds, hut-keepers, stockmen, and persons of this description, who would, if they should come amongst our people, be always in the way, and might do us incalculable mischief.

The Governor, again, in this case, heartily supported my application, and the sections in question were declared to be a Native Reserve. Then came the question of the run. I know that it would be quite too much to ask that the Government should purchase the sheep and run, and I therefore determined to make that purchase myself, that is to say, I induced my father to advance the money for me. I no doubt fully explained to him how my heart was set upon this enterprise, and I felt sure that he would help me in the matter. I therefore drew upon him for £1,200, and my bills were, in due course, readily accepted by him.

I must here explain that when a run having stock upon it changes hands, the stock, having been absolutely the property of the vendor, becomes absolutely the property of the purchaser, and the purchaser takes the place of the vendor as lessee of the run under the Government.

The run, known as the Poonindie run, is a most interesting and picturesque bit of country, on the shore of Louth Bay in Spencer's Gulf. The most prominent features are the River Tod and Mount Gawler. The last-named is a very pretty round-topped hill, rising perhaps about 300 ft. above the sea, and is excellent feeding ground throughout. The Tod is a very short tidal river, which ceases running during the dry weather in summer, but in the rainy season a large body of water is sometimes poured down from the sides of Mount Gawler, and the river becomes impassable at the ford. The river is at all times deep and of considerable width as far as the tide comes up, the banks being steep and well-defined.

It was at this part of the river, on a level, pleasant, grassy plain, that our little village was eventually placed and the river, with its deep water holes, for swimming and fishing, was a never-failing source of pleasure and occupation to the natives. The one drawback was that sandbanks, or shoals, barred the entrance from the sea, so that the river was of no use to us as regards our intercourse with the ships which brought our stores or took away our produce.

I am not sure of the extent of the run, but I think it was about twelve square miles. The important question, however, about a run is not so much—How big is it? as—What amount of stock will it carry? There were 3,400 sheep upon the run when I got it, and, with that number upon it, it was supposed to be fully stocked. The only building upon it near the Tod was a hut in a very dilapidated condition. It had, in fact, been seriously damaged by fire not long before I came into possession. (It was built of stone, with a mud floor.) We were, therefore, under the necessity of putting up all our own buildings, and this, as may be supposed, afforded abundant occupation for all hands for a long time. As regards our immediate wants in the way of shelter, after our experience on the island, we had very little difficulty in putting up temporary huts, similar to those which we had erected before. We therefore lost no time in getting about the permanent huts and other buildings for the natives and my white assistants. For myself and family, I rented a wooden house in the little township of Port Lincoln, until, other things having been attended to, I could get a dwelling for myself put up. In the meantime, I spent most of the week at Poonindie, sleeping sometimes in one place, sometimes in another, as the case might be. But I was always in Port Lincoln on the Sunday, where I held services regularly for the few Europeans who lived in the little township and the neighbourhood.

Now, about the sheep and my white helpers. Sheep in

Australia are not only valuable property, but they are also perishable property: that is to say, they are especially liable to injury if they are not very carefully watched and guarded by night as well as by day. I thought it would be very bad policy to expose them to any unnecessary risks, and therefore I retained the services of the European shepherds for some months, and I also engaged an overseer. The task of putting up substantial buildings also required more skill and knowledge than the natives possessed; and again, the natives were not, at first, skilled as farm labourers. So that in one way and another, I had several white men in my employ when we began to form our settlement. There was, however, plenty of work to be done which could be done by unskilled hands; so that there was no lack of employment for the natives. And, as will be seen as my narrative proceeds, they themselves very soon became skilled hands, and were able to take the place of the Europeans both in shepherding and in the cultivation of the soil.

My predecessor on the run—Mr. Spicer—had not attempted cultivation of any kind; but with us it was necessarily a matter of supreme importance that we should grow our own grain; and I began at once to prepare very energetically for the performance of this duty. Our first operations were, as may be supposed, on a comparatively small scale. Our first crop was harvested at the end of 1851, and it will be seen that we made pretty rapid progress when I state that the crop of the end of 1855 (the last harvested before my departure) yielded no less than 700 bushels of wheat of excellent quality,

I brought with me from Adelaide two horses and a spring cart, and I bought a pony from Mr. Spicer. These animals enabled us to keep up our communication with Port Lincoln, and the journeys between the two places were necessarily pretty frequent. We had to procure everything from that township. The post-office was there; and there came all communications with Adelaide and the rest of the world. But, although our light horses enabled us to keep up this communication, heavier animals became necessary when we began our building, fencing, &c., &c.

It would have been of no use to begin our cultivation until we had formed our paddocks, and protected them by proper fences. I was getting horned cattle on the run, as I found opportunity of buying good ones, and quiet; and nothing but post and rail fences would be sufficient to keep them off growing crops. These fences I had put up by white men, working by contract.

The overseer whom I first engaged was not a satisfactory person, and I kept him only a short time. The next was Mr. George Wollaston, one of the sons of the Venerable John Ramsden Wollaston, appointed first Archdeacon of Western Australia by Bishop Short (Western Australia having been included in the diocese of Adelaide). Mr. G. Wollaston understood the care of sheep and farming in all its branches, and gave me most valuable assistance in all my outdoor operations. He did all the ploughing the first season; the natives, of course, giving him all the assistance he required in looking after his teams, driving for him, &c.

Mr. Minchin's duties detained him more upon the premises amongst the huts. He kept school for the natives during school hours, and at other times had to look after those who were not engaged upon any fixed job. He had to see that there were none of them idling about, but that they were all doing something.

It was my duty to send regular reports to the Government, and I did send them, sometimes more fully, sometimes briefly. These reports were published in the Government Gazette, and are, of course, now accessible, if any one wishes to see them; I find that I have preserved a few of them, but not many.

I must here make mention of other reports which it was my duty to make; but which I fear I did not make except with great irregularity, viz., reports to S.P.G. The Society was extremely liberal to the Bishop on the first formation of the Diocese, and indeed for many years afterwards. I was one of its missionaries, and others of the clergy were greatly indebted to it for its bounty. I therefore ought to have sent in my reports with strict regularity; but, having duties of so many kinds upon my hands, I found that rendering my quarterly reports to the Government was as much as I could manage. It was, in fact, a serious tax upon my time and attention, and I fear my more lenient master, S.P.G., was rather badly treated in the matter of reports. From one of my reports to the Government, viz., that for June, 1851, I find that same periodical, which I have already made use of, has in its issue for August of that year made the following extracts. These extracts will serve to show what our position was at the above-named date, seven or eight months after we commenced operations :—

" By purchasing the sheep depasturing on the surrounding runs, I have acquired also the use of about 12 square miles as run ; so that, as far as locality is concerned, I consider that our advantages are very great. We have good (though not first-rate) agricultural land, good pasturage, abundance of fuel, and good water.

" The buildings at present consist of three substantial stone huts, and nine log huts.

" A well-manured paddock of five acres has been cleared, fenced with a three-rail fence, and sown with oats. A portion of another eighty-acre paddock is also being fenced and ploughed. Three wells have also been dug.

" These works have been carried on mostly by European agency. The natives are helpers, or (as the Archdeacon terms them) 'second-class labourers,' whom they have ' employed in a variety of ways ; and, thus employed (says he), they have worked with considerable steadiness, and have cheerfully performed their duties.'

"Their wages, in ordinary cases, are 6d. per day (of five hours), but for extra work they are paid more. These wages, it appears, they only draw as they require cash ; and when drawn, ' they *never* squander it, but lay it out in clothes or articles which may be useful about their houses.'

" Each couple reside at present in the small log huts, which they keep tidy, and ' make decided efforts to surround themselves with the comforts of civilised life.'

" The number of natives in residence at the Institution at the present time is fourteen ; four couples ; two single men, two single women, and two boys ; 19 in all have been sent to us from Adelaide. Of these, three have been dismissed and sent back to Adelaide, one out of five who have been to Adelaide on a visit, did not return, and one has died.'

" The Archdeacon considers the native school in Adelaide very desirable for first teaching our language and inculcating right principles and habits, as the impressions made in their early life will be the most durable.

" The amount of funds in aid of the Institution have been as follows :—Contributions in the Colony, about £80 ; from the public funds granted by his Excellency, £300.

" The agency at present consists of Mr. H. P. Minchin, Mr. G. Wollaston, Mr. W. Chandler, and Mrs. Smith."

I wish here to make some explanation about the cases of dismissal referred to in the above report. The object which I had primarily in view (and I always tried to have this clearly understood) was to *carry on* the instruction and training of those children, or young persons, who had been brought up in the Adelaide School. Those who, so to speak, had been thus handled by European teachers when they were young, had acquired, at any rate, *the idea* of being under control. I may go further and say that, as a matter of fact, they had acquired, not only the idea of order, but habits of order and obedience.

It was my purpose to try to induce those who were put under my care to go on training themselves in the habits of civilised life, and all my plans would have been defeated if I had allowed, especially in the first instance, the daily presence amongst us of those who had not acquired even the idea of obedience and of order. But, while I firmly declined to receive anyone who had not been in the Adelaide School, I was more than willing to receive back those who had simply outgrown the school, and had left it from no fault of their own. Some, who proved to be amongst our very best inmates and most efficient work-men, were young men who had been in the school, and had left it ; some for a considerable time. But, having been under the quieting, training, influence of school life in their early years, those who had any real desire to remain in the Institution, and were likely to be benefited by it, soon fell again into habits of obedience and order.

I remember quite well the three persons mentioned above as having been dismissed. Two of them were men. They had, apparently, associated with white men of a low class after they left the school and before they came to us. They gave us a great deal of trouble, and did much harm while they were with us ; and we found that matters went on much better and more quietly after they were sent away.

Upon the third case, that of a female, I must dwell at some length. Maria, the black girl at Government House, was known by repute to almost every one in Adelaide. The fact of her being an inmate of Government House, and the further fact of the remarkable progress which she had made towards civilization, combined to give her this general notoriety.

The Bishop and Mrs. Short were guests of Governor Robe for some time after our arrival, and the Bishop, writing to a friend in England, said :—" We have a native girl in " the house. She has been here five years ; and makes a " very good servant. She does our washing, and I am told " gets up linen very well; but I have not yet seen her " performance. If she is treated harshly, or offended, she " will walk off for a day or two, and then come back. And " I am told that, when the weather is very hot, she will " leave her clothes and throw a blanket over her shoulders " and go into the bush."

I get this out of a little book published by S.P.C.K., " Annals of the Colonial Church—Diocese of Adelaide." Nothing is said about the date of the letter, but I am of opinion that there is conclusive internal evidence that it was written soon after our arrival in Adelaide, say early in 1848. As I have already implied, Maria was a person much talked about, and many little incidents were repeated to illustrate her advancement towards civilization, and to show that she attached considerable importance to her attainments. For example, it was said that some young man once spoke to her in that jargon in which the uncultivated natives are usually spoken to. Whereupon Maria drew herself up and said, " Why do you talk to me like that ? I can speak English as well as you can."

Maria came to us in October, 1850, probably about two years and a half after the writing of the Bishop's letter. She had, unhappily, in the meantime, fallen into disreputable habits of life. But, as she was willing to join us, I was quite willing to receive her, hoping that she might retrieve her character, and become a respectable woman. She brought with her a little half-caste son about seven months old ; and partly on the child's account, and partly on her own account, she remained at first chiefly in our own house. But, we found after a time, that it was impossible to keep her. She conducted herself in such a way that it was quite certain that she was not trying to reform her own habits; and that she would, necessarily, do much harm as an inmate of the Institution. I kept her only about four months, and was then obliged to send her away. She was quite willing to leave her little son, and we were quite willing to keep him. He grew up to be a young man, and was drowned in a boat-accident in Louth Bay early in 1872.

This case of Maria, being so very widely known, became a stock case in the mouths of all persons who wished to throw cold water upon efforts to civilize and Christianize the natives. "Look at the case of Maria; think what was done for her! Think how everyone was led to suppose that that she was going to be a truly respectable woman. See now what has become of her: she has taken to bad ways, and has altogether gone wrong." Yes, but who led her into those bad ways? I have the authority of Mr. Moorhouse himsell for stating that the person who first led her astray was the proprietor of a thriving store in one of the best streets in Adelaide. He systematically laid siege to the girl, gave her presents, flattered and fed her vanity, and set her going upon her downward path. There was no reason why anything about the natives should be unknown to Mr. Moorhouse. From one or another of them he he could find out anything he wished to know.

The first death amongst the natives is referred to in this report, and, because it is the first mentioned, and because in the course of my narrative, many more will be mentioned, I desire to make some remarks on the subject of native mortality.

English readers, who know only about the rate of mortality in European countries, will be startled on learning how frequently deaths occurred amongst us. But everyone who knows even a little about aboriginal races is aware that those races which are of a low type mentally, and who are, at the same time, weak in constitution, rapidly die out when their country comes to be occupied by a different race much more vigorous, robust and pushing than themselves. The phenomenon is explained in many different ways, according to men's preconceived opinions and habits of thought. But, whatever may be the true explanation, there can be no doubt about the fact.

When I was making my final report to the Government on leaving the Institution, I asked our medical attendant—Dr. Lawson—to state, in writing, the result of his experience. He says :—

"I have had some thirteen years' professional experience "amongst the aborigines of this Colony.

"Having acted as medical attendant to the Native "Training Institution since its commencement in 1850, "and, having visited and prescribed for, I believe, every "case which has proved fatal, I can, with confidence, state "that the principal cause of death was of a pulmonary "character, in one form or other. The disease is very "common with natives (he means those in the bush): "*only their deaths are not particularly taken notice of, or even* "*inquired into.* Let the cause be as it may, once they are "attacked there is little or no hope of a recovery. This "has been proved at the Poonindie Institution, where they "have had all the comfort and attention that could be "given in such cases. They are by nature too weak, I may "say, to stand any disease."

This evidence is, of course, of infinitely more value than anything which I can say. But I must repeat here some remarks which I copy from my own printed report to the Government: "I fully admit that, as regards health and dura-"tion of life amongst our inmates, our efforts have not met "with that measure of success which I had hoped for and "expected. But whilst admitting this, I by no means admit "that the question of the utility of the Institution is "affected, except to a very limited extent, or that the duty "of maintaining it is affected at all. Health and duration "of life are unquestionably great and important objects in "this world, and great blessings when it pleases God to "grant them to us. But they are not the *chief objects* of "life. So far from these being the *chief objects* there are, "undoubtedly, many other objects which it is a man's duty "and also his interest to pursue, even though health and "duration of life be sacrificed in the pursuit."

With reference to the constitutional weakness of the natives I said, "In an unhealthy season, in which there "would be, amongst Europeans, an unusual prevalence of "sickness (as in influenza, &c.), but, perhaps, no unusual "number of deaths, the sickness amongst the natives would "assume a much more serious and deadly character, and

" the number of deaths amongst them would be very
" greatly increased."

With reference to the rapidity with which certain tribes
die out and disappear, I said as follows (and it must be
borne in mind that this was written in an official document
to be presented to the Government, with a view to its being
printed and published for general information. I was not
likely, therefore, to hazard such a statement as this without
being very certain that it was correct): " I may, as an
" instance, refer to the case of the tribe which formerly
" occupied the country whereon the city of Adelaide and
" the surrounding townships now stand. In 1836, as I
" have been repeatedly informed by old colonists, there
" dwelt in that country a numerous tribe. Fourteen years
" from that time, viz., in 1850, when my acquaintance
" with the natives commenced, that tribe was on the very
" verge of extinction. The members of it had, in that
" short time, become so few that, although I have received
" from Adelaide for this Institution sixty-seven individuals,
" six only belonged to the tribe I speak of. . . . I
" know also, from my own observation during my residence
" here, that the process of extinction amongst the natives
" of this district has been going on at a very rapid rate."

In consequence of this want of stamina, or the powers of
endurance, the working hours at Poonindie were much
shorter than the usual working hours of white men. From
five to six hours a day were our usual hours. I have no
doubt, however, that, at busy times, harvest time and
shearing time, the men worked very much longer. I am
quite aware that there might have been found many picked
men capable of enduring great fatigue. In almost every
exploring expedition the party would include probably two
natives, who, in some cases, rendered most important
services during the journey, and appeared to be equal to
the white men in their powers of endurance.

I have gone into this digression on the first mention of a
death amongst our inmates, because I am afraid that the
frequent mention of death, which will be found in my
narrative, might prove a serious stumbling block to some
of my readers. My purpose is not only to mention the
deaths as they occur, but, in some cases, to dwell on them.

It is unhappily the habit of the ordinary unthinking colonial man (I am speaking of white men) to look upon, and to

treat, the natives as scarcely human beings. They seem to think that they are found in the land to be treated and made use of merely as beasts of burden. The idea of the possibility of these natives becoming Christians never enters into the minds of the white men of the class I speak of. What I want to show is that not only can they become Christians, but they can become Christians of a very high order measured by the true standard of Christianity. They can receive the Truths of Christianity with that mind most dear to our blessed Lord—the mind of the little child, with its meekness and docility and truthfulness, and they can go on growing in grace, responding in their lives to the exhortation set before the Christians at Rome, "rejoicing " in hope, patient in tribulation, continuing constant in " prayer."

In making this digression, I have anticipated somewhat in time ; but we are still engagd with the events of 1851. We had only the one death in that year; and the movement amongst the natives in favour of Christianity had not yet commenced.

Early in the year some of our leading men went to Adelaide for an outing. They had been scholars in one of the Church Sunday Schools in Adelaide, and by this and other means they had many friends and acquaintances. There were also many other friends of the Institution who were glad to see them. First and foremost amongst those friends were the Bishop and Mrs. Short, who were always most kind and hospitable to them. Such visits to the chief city did good to the men themselves, and they did good also to the Institution.

It was by means of such visits that we got back many of those, of whom I have already spoken, who had left the school and had gone elsewhere. The news quickly spread that some Poonindie boys (they were always spoken of as boys) were in Adelaide, well dressed, and made much of by the white people, and that they liked Poonindie, and were going back. Old schoolmates came in to see them ; and, as I have just said, several were thus restored to civilization who had wandered away. The white friends had nothing but what was good to say of the conduct and manners of their black visitors ; and the latter returned to their homes and to their work at the appointed time, bringing with them sometimes one, sometimes two or three recruits.

Amongst the many duties which engaged our attention when we first took possession of our run was the duty of tracing and marking the boundaries thereof. Mr. Spicer and the white shepherds had, no doubt, a general knowledge of the boundaries such as answered their purposes. But, for various reasons, it was absolutely necessary that we should have those boundaries distinctly marked. And this could be done only by a professional surveyor. The person who rendered this service to us was John Macdougal Stuart, afterwards known to fame as the able and daring explorer who crossed the Australian Continent from South to North, and planted the Union Jack on the sea shore on the northern coast. The track which he laid down in the chart became, a few years afterwards, the telegraph line from Adelaide to Port Darwin.

The affairs of the Institution, negotiations with the Government, &c., &c., made it necessary for me to go to Adelaide from time to time. Moreover, I could not rightly separate myself altogether from diocesan affairs. I, therefore, paid two or three visits to our chief city in the course of 1851. The distance was about 200 miles by sea, and our passenger vessel was a small schooner of about 30 tons. If the wind and weather happened to be fair the passage either way was not so bad. Sometimes we had anything but fair weather, and then the knocking about in the little craft was miserable enough.

Sometimes the wind would blow persistently for several days from one quarter ; and when the persistent wind blew from an unfavourable quarter a start would be postponed from day to day in the most trying manner, intending passengers being obliged to remain in the township, or run the risk of losing the passage.

I was detained in Adelaide in this way in the month of September in this year. A neighbour who lived near to Poonindie, and, with whom I was very intimate, Mr. William Peter, was detained in the same way. (He has been now, for many years, a prosperous settler in New Zealand, and a member of the Upper House of the Legislature.) He became very impatient in consequence of the delay and the great waste of time. At last he could stand it no longer, and determined to go overland round the head of Spencer's Gulf; and I agreed to go with him. I had to furnish myself with everything for the journey—horse, saddle and bridle, tether rope and hobbles, saddle bags, &c., &c. However, we soon made our preparations, and started on the 11th of September.

I find the following entry made in my diary at Port Lincoln in the same year, under date July 23rd, making mention of the same journey made by four police troopers. When I made the entry I little thought that I should so soon make the journey myself.

" July 23rd :—This evening arrived the four policemen, " who left Adelaide June 25th, to travel overland round the " head of the gulf. They were thus twenty-seven days on " their journey. At one period of their journey, something " north of Franklin Harbour, they suffered much through " the want of water. Their provisions also ran short, as " they started with only ten day's rations."

They would not have to use their own rations at the beginning of the journey, as they would make police stations at night.

" Mr. Dashwood expected that they would accomplish " the journey in fourteen days, which I told him I was con- " fident they would not do. People who know the route " consider that Mr. Eyre performed a feat in getting round " in 1842 in seventeen days."

From the 11th of September to the 21st we were travelling through settled country, within the colony of South Australia, on the eastern side of the Gulf. We stayed every night at stations, and were most hospitably entertained. On the 21st we took leave of inhabited country, and from that day to the 28th, we had to depend upon the scanty stock of provisions which we were able to carry on our one pack horse. At that time no human habitation existed down the whole western side of the Gulf; and until we reached Port Lincoln District, we did not see a single human being, either white or black. The want of water for our horses was the great difficulty. We could carry a little for ourselves, but the horses could get a drink only when we came to some scanty spring or puddle of rain water in a hole in a rock or a clay-pan. Upon one occasion, apparently about the same part of the journey as that in which the four policemen suffered, we were forty hours without water for the horses, and they had to travel fifty-five miles during that time.

We were accompanied by a man who had been in the

police, but had left the force. He generally lead the pack horse. But our path-finder was Mr. Peter, who had, in a very remarkable degree, the valuable faculty of never being at a loss about his whereabouts in the bush. I am told that there have now, for many years, been thriving sheep stations all down the west side of Spencer's Gulf.

As my readers will have supposed the schooner, for whose departure we had waited in Adelaide, arrived at Port Lincoln before us. But we had had a most interesting journey. I was, in colonial phrase, almost a "new chum" in the Colony, having been out not quite three years, and the novelty of the thing charmed me greatly. I had really enjoyed the journey ; and I have always looked back upon it with great satisfaction, as one of the marked events of my life.

By this time (the end of September), Mr. Wollaston, considering the many things which had to be attended to, had made good progress with the cultivation. He had ploughed and sown about eleven or twelve acres. But the crops, this first season, were, I think, all cut for hay. I think no corn was grown until the season of 1852.

Our sheep shearing began on the 8th of October, and was finished on the 28th. Eleven bales of wool were sent away on the 16th, but I find no record of the number of bales which were sent away altogether. And I cannot say positively whether any of the natives took part in the actual shearing. But as I certainly intended that they should be shearers, I think it highly improbable that I should have let the opportunity pass by without setting some of them on to learn.

During the month of November our operations suffered some hindrance in consequence of a Mr. Hayes having induced the Government to send me a requisition to assist him in making some experiments in charcoal burning. Mr. Hayes arrived November 6th, with his apparatus, which was a large retort. I have no memo. of its size, but, so far as I remember, it was about 6 or 7 feet in length, and nearly, or quite, 3 feet in diameter. This had to be mounted upon masonry in such a way that a large fire might be kept burning underneath.

A mason was hired to do the stone work, but the labour connected with the operation was considerable, and our teams and men were in this way occupied for several days. The retort had to be got up from the beach ; the stone for the building had to be carted to the place selected for the experiments; much wood had to be cut and carted, some for consumption in the retort, and some for the fire underneath. The operation was to answer two purposes: the extraction of a liquid from the wood within the retort, and the reduction of the wood itself to charcoal. We began at once to make preparations, and on the 11th we had got the retort and other parts of the apparatus to the scene of operations. On the 18th the first charge was drawn and it was not a success. The wood in the retort was not properly burned, so another charge was drawn the next day, and the note in my diary is that the wood was properly burned, but that the burning had taken 18 or 19 hours; a much longer time than Mr. Hayes had led us to expect. He seemed to attach considerable importance to the liquid extracted; but I have no note about it, and I do not remember what became of it.

I now told Mr. Hayes that, having by means of our labour given him a fair opportunity of trying his experiment, I must leave him to take his own course; but that we must put our own men to our own work. He felt much aggrieved, and appealed to the Government. But I pointed out to him that his demand that we should leave our own urgent work in order to please him was most unreasonable. What representations he made to the Government I don't know; but he entirely failed to show that his experiments,. even if they had answered his expectations, would have been of any service to anyone. There was no market for the charcoal. A blacksmith living about five miles off took some of it, but he attached no importance to it. It would answer his purpose better to burn his own charcoal nearer home. Mr. Hayes could have hired other men to continue his operations if he had chosen to do so. But he did nothing more.

After this, Mr. Wollaston and some of the natives took a trip to Adelaide. They left November 20th, and returned December 6th, bringing more recruits with them.

At the end of December I had occasion to go to Adelaide myself, and upon this occasion our voyage caused, at one time, very considerable anxiety. In fact, we were in great danger. During a heavy squall, just when we were passing the Althorpe Islands, the light in the binnacle was blown out. The man at the helm (the captain) could not see the compass, and, of course, could not tell how the little craft was heading, or what she was doing. The wind continued to blow hard, and the captain seemed to us to be a long time fumbling with his lamp before he could secure it properly, and keep it alight. We were very thankful, however, that he made it all right at last, and we pursued our course.

The last illness and death of Takan-arro, which I am now about to describe, had a most important bearing upon my proceedings. Not my own mind only, but many minds were deeply stirred by this event. It had a great effect upon the minds of the natives in the school, and gave a great impetus to the desire to go to Poonindie. I had desired to be cautious in my admissions to the Institution; but I now consented to receive several new candidates, and I took them with me on my return.

Before I proceed with the story of Takan-arro, I must say something about Mr. Moorhouse and Mr. Ross. I have already mentioned Mr. Moorhouse as the Protector of Aborigines, appointed by the Government. He was a fully qualified medical practitioner, and had had, in that capacity, much experience amongst the natives. The interest which he took in Takan-arro's spiritual state, shows him to have been a truly good man. This he certainly was, and the assistance which he gave to me at all times was of the greatest importance to me. His house was very near to the Native School. Mr. Ross was the schoolmaster, also a truly good man—and there can be no doubt but that his teaching was the means chiefly employed by God to bring Takan-arro to that blessed state of mind in which I found him. It gives me pleasure to testify to the immense advantage which it was to me, in dealing with those who had been at the school, that they had had, in their early years, such a good and godly instructor as Mr. Ross.

SOME ACCOUNT OF THE LAST ILLNESS AND DEATH OF TAKAN-ARRO,

A CHRISTIAN ABORIGINAL NATIVE OF SOUTH AUSTRALIA.

[The following extract is taken from the Diary of the Venerable ...w B. Hale, M.A., Archdeacon of Adelaide, and Missionary ...ndent of the Native Training Institution at Port Lincoln. ...unt of the Institution, see *Annals of the Diocese of* ...59.]

... 30th, 1851.—When visiting the Natives' ...his day, Mr. Ross told me that one of

D

the lads was very ill, that, in fact, he was not expected to recover. He said he was one of their best boys; and, when he mentioned his name, Takan-arro, I at once remembered him as being one of the candidates for admission into our Institution, and also as one of the most promising of the native boys attending the Sunday-school of St. John's. Mr. Ross told me that during the first part of his illness he had been at Mr. Moorhouse's residence, and that he (Mr. M.) had been much gratified by the indications which he had given of seriousness of mind and hopes of a better world. When I saw Mr. Moorhouse, he also told me, that in the early stage of his illness, when not so weak as at present, he had been very diligent in reading the New Testament, for which part of the Bible he expressed his preference, because it told him about Jesus Christ. Mr. Moorhouse had more than once heard him praying earnestly when by himself, and for this purpose he would even raise himself up in his bed during the night. He had also requested to have read to him a particular chapter, the hearing of which gave him special pleasure, viz., 1 John iii. beginning " Behold what manner of love." The expectations and hopes which I had formed respecting him were fully realised when I had the happiness of hearing him speak for himself. His expressions with regard to the forgiveness of his sins and his trust in Jesus Christ, were most gratifying and satisfactory. He was very importunate to be taken with me to Port Lincoln ; nor could I, for some time, make him desist from his entreaties, which he urged even with tears. I reminded him again and again of his extreme weakness, and the impossibility of his being removed : but he still kept on, " I want to go with you ; you stay two or three days." Then he said, " All my boys gone away to Port Lincoln—Tartuan and Mudlong and Kadling-arro and Kandwillan ; I want to see my boys." Then I reminded him that he had better pray to God to forgive him his sins and make him a good boy, and take him to a better place ; and that I hoped those boys would do the same and be good ; and then they would all meet again and would never be parted any more, nor have sickness nor pain. I promised moreover, that if it should please God to make him well again he should go to Port Lincoln. I asked him about his prayers—if he pray much, and he said he used to pray more when h

Mr. Moorhouse's, but now he was *so weak*. When I prayed with him he joined very fervently in the prayers, and repeated the petitions of the Lord's Prayer and other petitions after me with great earnestness. After remaining with him for some time, I went into Mr. Moorhouse's office. Whilst I was there Mr. Ross came to me and said that Takan-arro wanted to see me again to pray with him. His particular object in sending for me was, that I might repeat with him the general Confession; as that being familiar to his mind, he could follow me more readily. I did so accordingly, and he repeated it after me in the most solemn and fervent manner. I had now further conversation with him, and became more and more satisfied as to the reality and depth of his religious feelings, and the question came forcibly home to me—What doth hinder him from being baptised? I therefore went again to Mr. Moorhouse, to ascertain from him what he really thought of the probability of life being continued to him for any length of time. Mr. M. said he had no hope of his recovery; that he might live a few days, or he might go off suddenly—even that very night. I then deemed it right to baptize him without delay. I recapitulated to him, in a few plain words, the nature and intent of that Holy Sacrament; and he expressed his desire to receive it. Mr. Ross then came in, as did also one of our own Institution boys, now visiting Adelaide—Pitpanure—and, with great joy, I admitted this child of the desert into the communion and fellowship of the saints. When I once more took leave of him and was going out, followed by Pitpanure, he called after the latter, and said, " I want him stay pray with me." Pitpanure readily consented to remain, and seemed much impressed at the whole scene. In the course of many years of close and constant attendance at the bedside of the sick and dying, seldom have I been more affected, and, I may also say, more edified, than I was this day by the bedside of this poor native.

Wednesday, December 31st.—This morning I found him less languid and apparently better. He spoke in the same edifying manner as before. I asked him if he had been able to pray ; and he said that he had awoke in " the dark time," and had called Pitpanure and asked him to pray with him. His answers, with respect to his desire for for-

giveness, his trust in Jesus Christ, and his hopes of heaven, were given in the same ready and satisfactory manner as before ; and he followed me most fervently when praying. He seemed more at ease and peaceful than yesterday, and I asked him if he was happy. He said—Yes, he was happy. Pitpanure is most constant and tender in waiting upon him. I asked him how he had slept, and if he was comfortable ; and he described to me how Pitpanure had got up and arranged his bed and made it softer for him.

I saw him three or four times in the course of the day. His Sunday School teacher also came to see him and talked with him.

Thursday, January 1st, 1852.—Having been occupied out of town this morning, it was about one o'clock when I arrived at the Native School. Mr. Ross told me that Takan-arro was not so well, and was then asleep ; that he had asked repeatedly for me. I was unwilling to disturb him from his sleep, and went away, saying I would return to see him. When I returned it was about four o'clock. Mr. Ross said he had not been at all pleased that I had gone away without waking him. When I talked to him, his expressions as to the state of his mind were, to the full, as satisfactory and pleasing as upon the previous days. He said he had not been able to pray so well because he had been *so weak*. When I led him in prayer he joined as earnestly and fervently as before. I again read the general Confession for this purpose, for the reasons before given, offering up also other short and plain petitions, such as he could well appreciate. As I directed his mind to profitable contemplations, he spoke with considerable freedom and intelligence, and manifested the greatest earnestness and attention. For instance, the lads at the school had been more away from him to-day than on the previous days, and he expressed a feeling of loneliness. I then reminded him of the condition of the Saviour when in the hands of his enemies, how "all His disciples forsook Him and fled ;" and again, how the three had slept in the garden instead of watching with Him whilst He prayed. He perfectly entered into the application of these lessons, and repeated some of the disciples' names and mentioned the part they had taken in these transactions. Again, on speaking to him about sorrow for sin, I asked him to recollect something particular which he had done wrong and for which

he was now sorry. Then he said, after a little pause, "I remember, a long time ago, when some other boys tempted me and I went with them into a garden and took some melons; " and then he added two or three times, with great earnestness, "but I won't do it again—I won't do it again." He was extremely unwilling for me to leave him; and, more than once, when I had risen from my seat, he would have me sit down again, saying, "You are not going away yet." He was very particular in getting my promise to visit him again on the morrow.

Friday, January 2nd.—When I went in to see him to-day, I found the Bishop [of Adelaide] with him. He was sitting up, and appeared better than yesterday—much less weak and languid. The Bishop, when I went in, was recalling to his mind the chief passages of Scripture which speak of the second coming of Christ; and the glorified form which will be worn upon that occasion by Himself and His people; and thence referring to the Transfiguration on the Mount. His answers and manner were such as to show that his mind was fully alive to all that was being said, and he listened with the greatest interest and attention. The Bishop afterwards expressed to me his surprise, as well as his extreme pleasure and gratification, in having witnessed the degree of intellingence which he displayed, and the earnest manner in which he entered into the subject. Mr. Moorhouse, who was also present, told me, that before I arrived, he had been saying that he believed if he should die he should go to heaven, where Jesus Christ is, and that he should be happy there. Upon this occasion, also, Mr. Moorhouse remarked upon the vivacity of mind which he habitually exhibited in reference to spiritual things: that his attention is always alive to these matters—that, when-ever you go to him, you find that these are the subjects uppermost in his thoughts—and that he always takes pleasure in hearing about them. This testimony from Mr. Moorhouse as to this point is very important, because, being near at hand, he is in and out with him more frequently than I am. I found him quite full of these subjects when I began to talk to him : he had the Testament on one side of him on the bench, and the Book of Common Prayer on the other side; in each of these books he had marked a passage which had especially arrested his attention whilst reading by himself, and which he wished to point out to me. In the Testament he had marked 1 John v., and in the Prayer Book, the Gospel for the Fourth Sunday in Lent, viz., part of John vi. In conversation he showed himself even more to advantage than on the previous days; partly, no doubt, in consequence of his feeling stronger and better bodily. He talked and answered questions put to him with great earnestness and intelligence. He told me that Pitpanure and he had again got up in the night to pray; and that they had also prayed together this morning. He said that he felt that whatever God should see fit to do with him would be good; whether to take him to a better place, or to return him to health and continue his life in this world. He felt that he was quite satisfied te leave the matter entirely in God's hands.

Saturday, January 3rd.—To-day he appeared much weaker again, and his mind and intellectual powers seemed to participate in this want of energy and tone. Mr. Moorhouse considers him much weaker than yesterday. As regards his spiritual state, praised be God, I can affirm that every time I see him I am more and more satisfied as to his concern about the one thing needful, and that he has a deep and heartfelt desire to be a true and faithful follower of the Lord Jesus.

Sunday, January 4th.—When I visited him to-day he appeared rather more lively again than he had been yesterday. Mr. Moorhouse, however, does not think at all more favourably of him, as to the probability of his recovery. I asked him if anything particularly occurred to him which he wished me to read from the Scripture, and he said, "About Christ upon the cross." When I was leaving him I met the Bishop (who had been at the hospital and the Pulteney-street schoolroom) just coming to see him. As I had been with him some time, the Bishop said he would just see how he was, and speak two or three words to him. When, however, he was going out again, Takan-arro could not be contented that he should depart without first praying with him. "I want to pray with him," he said to me, in a tone of voice which indicated that he was yearning to lift his heart up in prayer to his blessed Saviour. The Bishop had been talking to him about the promised happiness of heaven, and the good men (Bible characters and others) who have already gone there; and he inquired if he should see those good men, and if he should know them. The Bishop also talked to him about his own people, upon which he seemed downcast, and was slow in entering into the subject. After a time he shook his head with an air of sadness, and said they were all upon the Murray. When the Bishop made further allusion to their state, and reminded him that he should pray for them, he said, " I like to teach them." The earnestness and fervency with which he joins in the prayers and responses to the petitions is at all times very striking, and this was especially the case to-day, both when I prayed with him, and also when the Bishop did so at his own particular request. The recollection of its being Sunday was quite upon his mind, and whilst I was sitting with him he two or three times expressed his wish that he had been able to go down to church. I asked him if, when the clergyman is speaking in church, he is able to understand him, and he said " Yes."

Wednesday, January 7th.—During the last three days he has been getting very much weaker, and more lethargic, so that he has lost, in a great degree, that vivacity of mind which was so remarkable upon previous occasions. Nevertheless, blessed be God, what he does say is all of the same peaceful and happy character as before. The manifestations of feeling are less strong, but still they are the same manifestations, and the feelings are the same. Yesterday and to-day I spoke to him with great plainness as to the probable very near approach of his death. He expressed no other feeling than that of resignation, and hope, and peace of mind at this prospect. He betrayed no wish for any other lot or dispensation of Providence than that which appeared to be prepared for him. He expressed his belief that his sins would be forgiven him, and that he should be happy with Christ his Saviour.

Thursday, January 8th.—I saw Takan-arro no more alive after making the preceding entry. I went to the Natives' School about 4 o'clock this day, when I learnt from Mr. Ross that he had departed to a better world about an hour before. He had not spoken since about nine o'clock in the morning. Death had been disarmed of all its terrors ere it visited him ; he had fallen asleep in Jesus with as much quietness and peace as the weary child would fall asleep in its mother's lap. The still, calm features, as I gazed upon them, seemed to testify, even in death, to that peace of God which, through divine goodness, had been mercifully shed abroad in his heart in life.

Friday, January 9th.—At a little past four o'clock this day, the Bishop and myself, Mr. Moorhouse, Mr. Ross, Pitpanure, and several of the native children now at the school, stood round a grave in the public cemetery, and committed to the earth, with the thrilling words of our Service for the Burial of the Dead, the mortal remains of the once wild and heathen Takan-arro. I read the service, and the Bishop addressed a few plain and impressive words to the native children. They have followed the corpse of their companion to its last-resting place on earth—God grant that many of this outcast people may follow his soul to its eternal resting-place above!

1852.—I left Adelaide again for Port Lincoln in the Government schooner *Yatala*, taking with me fifteen fresh volunteers from the school. The members of this party turned out extremely well; some of them became efficient leaders in our little community. The case of one of these was so peculiar that I must state some of the facts.

On the occasion of my visit to Adelaide in August and September, when our settlement had been for some months in existence, and, no doubt, much talked about amongst the natives generally, the transaction of my business on behalf of the Institution made it necessary for me to be much about the town of Adelaide, going in and out of stores, &c. Whilst thus engaged, I was constantly followed by a tall, powerful native lad, clad like the bush natives, *i.e.*, having simply his blanket thrown over his shoulder and wrapped round him. In answer to my inquiry as to what he wanted, the reply was, " Me want to go with you." I told him, again and again, that I could not take him—that Poonindie was only for those who had been in the school. Still he was not discouraged; wherever I went, and however long I might stay in any store or shop, there was the youth waiting, gazing upon me with an imploring look. He was not importunate or troublesome; but a look of earnest entreaty lighted up his black face whenever I gave him an opportunity of speaking—" Want to go with you." After a time this changed to " Me go to school."

This was a new view of the case. In the first place, I could not tell whether this great fellow, nearly six feet high, and, to all outward appearance, a mere wild black fellow, would be admitted to the school. In the next place, was it likely that he, having known no restraint in his younger days, being now probably of the age of about seventeen or eighteen, would conform to the rules of the school? However, I endeavoured to explain to him what going to school would mean : that he would have to sit quietly and obediently amongst the children, and try to learn lessons, &c. He most readily promised compliance with any commands which might be given to him ; and his anxiety about the matter was so great that I pleaded his cause, and obtained his admission to the school. He kept his promises and gave no trouble, and when I took away the party, some four months afterwards, my friend, Neruid, was a member of it. As his frame filled out he became physically a remarkably fine man, well proportioned, and, I may say, graceful in his movements. His feelings of affection for and gratitude to me were unmistakable. My least word was ever law to him, and from his height and strength and skill in labour of all kinds he became a most valuable member of our little society. He was baptized August 6th, 1853, and was a most consistent Christian all the time I was at Poonindie. He lived in that quiet Christian village for twenty years, dying February 9th, 1871.

His was the last death that had occurred when I re-visited the Institution in November, 1872. Four of the inmates of the Institution, seniors of it, in fact, having heard that I was likely to pay them a visit, wrote to me in July, 1872. Their letter contains these words : " Dear Father, " we have not forgotten you, although we have been parted " for many years and all our dear friends are gone, we " hope, to heaven. The last one God took away from " amongst us was our dear friend Charlie Neruid, and he " died believing in Christ, and he has left us a good " example." This is word for word, but I have, in a few instances, corrected the spelling.

The expression of a hope that their companion had gone to heaven is not to be viewed in the same light as similar expressions sometimes, unhappily, uttered in a light and careless manner by thoughtless persons of our own race. The tone of mind prevailing at Poonindie with reference to religion was intensely serious, and it was such that religious matters formed topics frequently talked about, so that, whatever a man's life might have been, it would have been difficult for him to be altogether unconscious as to whether he was living for heaven or not, and the simple-minded people were much too matter-of-fact to say lightly that their departed friends had gone to heaven, unless they had known by experience that they had been living for heaven.

The Bishop himself, writing to S.P.G., under date February 13th, 1857, says :—" Since Archdeacon Hale " left the Mission for Western Australia, seven months " ago, thirteen natives have died, some of them the most " advanced in intellect and spirit. In every instance, " save one, Mr. Hammond is satisfied that they died *in* " *hope*, and many in clear faith."

I must not, however, dismiss the subject of Neruid without mentioning a remarkable instance of the power of conscience, even in the mind of an Australian native. One means by which I expressed my displeasure in the case of any serious misconduct was by ordering the offender to confine himself to his hut, and not to mix with his companions until I should give him permission. Upon a certain occasion Neruid had sinned in thought and intention, and had also tempted one of his companions to sin. The sin, however, had not been actually committed, and there was no probability whatever that the matter would have come to my knowledge. But a reaction had set in in Neruid's mind, and he was filled with remorse. He confined himself to his hut of his own accord, and sent to me to tell me he wished to see me. When I went to him he told me, with every indication of the most sincere penitence, what was troubling his mind.

The considerable addition to our numbers, which I have already mentioned, necessarily increased our cares and anxieties. The new comers were mostly boys and lads, and arrangements had to be made for their superintendence while at work, and also for carrying on their school instruction. Mr. Minchin had been chiefly responsible for the school work ; but he was now chiefly employed in looking after those natives who were occupied in all kinds of miscellaneous work and odd jobs. And I engaged a fresh schoolmaster to carry on the reading and writing, &c.

Mr. Minchin's occupation was, at times, very trying,

and his services were of great value to the Institution. I find that in one of my reports to the Government I made mention of him in the following terms:—" It gives me the " most heartfelt pleasure to inform you that Mr. H. Paul " Minchin, who in the first instance entered so warmly " upon the work, has continued from that time to labour " in the cause with the most devoted zeal. Upon him has " fallen, in a great degree, the real drudgery of the under- " taking. While my part has been to exercise a general " supervision over the whole, his part has been to feel the " weight of the difficulties, and to stand at his post sup- " ported by his patience and his faith."

As we had some fair agricultural land, the raising of grain crops for our own maintenance was naturally a matter of primary importance. In the season of 1851 all the ploughing and sowing was done by Mr. Wollaston. But the gold fever was by this time at its height in Adelaide. Two of Mr. Wollaston's brothers had gone to the diggings, and they persuaded him to join them. He left early in March, 1852, and I had then no other alternative but to turn to myself, and train the natives to do all the agricultural work. Our efforts, I am happy to say, were crowned with success. We broke up several acres of fresh land, and had an excellent crop of wheat. The work was done entirely by the natives, with no other teaching except that which I could give them; and I had to be a learner myself. I had to get what information I required from books, and I then had to reduce it to practice in order to become a teacher. I shall, as I go on, give some extracts from my diary; and I shall give some explanations for the information of those readers who are not acquainted with the details of Australian farming.

I must here mention an event of no little importance to my own personal comfort. I have already stated that, when I brought my family from Adelaide, I took, for their accommodation, a wooden house in the little township of Port Lincoln. I myself went to and fro, spending most of the week at Poonindie; but being always at Port Lincoln on the Sunday. The getting up the necessary buildings (such as they were) for the Institution was a long and difficult task, and it was not until April, 1852, that I was able to get finished, and fit for our reception, a weather board house in the midst of the native village. Into this house I moved my family April 21, 1852. It was, of course, a great comfort to us all to be once more together, and it was a great help to me in my work to have my fixed dwelling at the station. I still continued to go into Port Lincoln for the Sunday services. Happily, I had in Port Lincoln, what I may almost call a second home in the house of my dear kind friends Captain and Mrs. Bishop, with whom I invariably stayed when I went into the township.

We had plenty of stone near at hand at Poonindie, but it was all of one kind : very hard water-worn boulders of all sizes collected from the bed of the river. Bricks were therefore an absolute necessity, and I engaged a professional brickmaker in Adelaide. By the latter end of March he had moulded enough for a kiln of 20,000. He had the assistance of such of the natives as he required ; and one or two became quite expert moulders. Much hauling of wood was requisite for the burning. This was done by the natives with bullock teams. In fact, hauling for one purpose or another was almost always going on, and, in addition to a team which I had already acquired by purchasing a few head of quiet cattle, I bought, towards the end of March, a team of eight bullocks with their dray and all their gear. These were sold to me at a very low price by a man bent upon going to the gold diggings, and we were now in a good position to begin ploughing whenever the rains should commence to render the ground sufficiently soft—until the rains commence, the ground, baked by the Australian summer, is quite impenetrable. We began ploughing on the 10th of March—the ground, however, was not sufficiently moistened for good work, and the work was therefore very trying to the new learners. I find this entry in my diary under the date just named. " This " attempt at ploughing, with the natives only as agents I " look upon as a most important event in its probable bear- " ing upon our future operations." In order to encourage them and to induce them to go on with spirit, I took the plough in hand myself. On March 25th I recorded as follows :—" I yoked up a pair of bullocks to-day for the first " time. Last week, for the first time, I succeeded in holding " the plough, and making tolerable work." On May 21 I recorded " This morning we had two teams of bullocks " again and made an excellent day's work. William held

" one plough and I the other (the iron one) the whole day."
These performances of mine, however, were only now and
again, and were of no real assistance to the men except as
an example and encouragement.

In my concise official report to the Government, dated
Dec. 31, 1852, I made the following statement: " With
" respect to the conduct of the natives generally, it gives
" me pleasure to speak of it in the same favourable terms
" as upon former occasions, and also as to the readiness
" with which they are brought to the performance of all
" kinds of ordinary labour. Our grain crop, grown entirely
" by them, has been, I am thankful to say, an abundant
" one, and, as the season is remarkably early, it has been
" already gathered in and stacked. With respect to the
" shearing of sheep (an operation still more difficult than
" those of either ploughing or reaping), not only were our
" own sheep shorn by the natives, but I was also able to
" undertake to shear for two other persons in the district.
" Our shearers went from home to shear for both these
" persons, and accomplished their work in a manner
" which would have done credit to any party of shearers of
" our own race."

But before I pass on to the next year, I must mention
some further particulars about our proceedings in 1852.
I stated above that when I took delivery of the sheep
I did not venture at first to put them under the care of
our own men. I retained, until the beginning of April,
the services of the white shepherds whom I found upon
the run. Certain of our own men were constantly with
those shepherds, and received instruction also from Mr.
Wollaston: so that by the time just named (April, 1852)
I was able to dispense with the white shepherds' services,
and our flocks were put entirely under the care of our own
men.

In saying this I must, however, except the lambing
season. This was in the month of June, when the rainy
season had fully set in. It is so critical a time for the
sheep, and a period of such immense importance, that I
considered it necessary to employ a competent white man
to give a general superintendence to the lambing. Several
of our own men were, however, necessarily employed,
giving him assistance and gaining experience for themselves. When the lambs had grown strong and the counting

time had arrived, it was found that we had an increase of 800.

Persons who are not acquainted with Australian sheep farming may wonder why the lambing is so timed as to fall in the midst of the rainy season. The reason is this : During the long and hot summer the country where the flocks feed becomes almost completely bare, and it is, therefore, peremptorily necessary to delay the lambing until, under the influence of the first rains, the young grass has sprung up sufficiently to afford the sheep the requisite nourishment. If the summer drought in any season continues much beyond the usual time, the sheep become so poor and weak that, if the lambing then commences, the mothers are not able to give the lambs the necessary nourishment, and a considerable portion of them die. No doubt wet and cold days and nights are very bad for the lambs, but starvation is still worse.

I identified myself with all the pursuits and proceedings of our inmates, and I did this not only as a policy— it was quite in accordance with my inclination. I liked to be associated with the men in their work, as well as in their recreation. I stood aloof from nothing. I took to bullock driving as well as ploughing. We were nothing without our bullocks. Their contribution towards our success was most important. My readers will therefore, I hope, permit me to devote a small space to these most useful animals. As with all inferior creatures which give their services to man, the behaviour of bullocks depends entirely upon the treatment which they receive.

White bullock-drivers in the Colonies are, unhappily, too often rough, drinking men, who have little idea of what can be done with animals by kindness and gentleness. The lash of their whips is for ever sounding on the poor brutes' backs, and the men seem to think that their language to them must necessarily be freely interspersed with oaths. The animals are often dazed and bewildered by their rough usage, and become awkward and difficult to manage. The manner of our drivers was all kindness and good temper, and the result was that our bullocks were quiet, obedient, and handy in the extreme. I confess that I took the greatest interest in them ; and I was soon able to handle them. In my diary, under date April 28th, 1852, I find this entry, " This morning, while

" Jack was absent looking for some bullocks, and Charley "in a different direction, I yoked up a team of six bullocks "and put them into the dray, the first time I have ac- "complished this feat myself. The dray was used for " hauling stone for Tom Coffin." Tom Coffin was the mason, and I presume there was a danger of his being hindered in his work for want of stone, and that there- fore I was anxious to get the dray ready, that the absent drivers might start for their work at once when they returned.

I do not know if I am right, but my impression is that when bullocks are used in England, they are always harnessed. I will, therefore, take the liberty of describing what " yoking up " means. All the gear that is put upon a bullock is simply the yoke and the bow. The yoke is a piece of wood long enough to be laid upon the necks of two bullocks standing side by side. The top is flat and the bottom slightly arched over the neck of each bullock to make it ride more easily. And it has, in it, four holes to receive the bows.

We will suppose, then, that six bullocks are to be yoked up. The driver puts them into a yard. As a rule, every bullock has his own place in the team, and they are much more easily brought up to be yoked, and they stand more steadily if the proper mates are brought up together. The pair which the driver means to yoke up first, he puts into a corner, their faces being against the rails of one side of the yard. He then, having the yoke and bows belonging to this pair at hand, stands on the near or left hand side of the animals, and, as gently and quietly as he can, puts the yoke across the two necks. Then he takes the bows, one after another, and pushes them up from below into, and through, the holes in the yoke intended for them.

The bows are then secured by small pieces of iron called keys. He then proceeds exactly in the same manner with the other two pairs. Having done this, he next places the three pairs in their proper order one behind the other against one side of the yard, having, as before, rails in front of them. Then he puts on the chains. Each yoke has a ring in the middle, to which the chain is hooked. The first pair are joined by the chain to the second pair, and another chain joins the second to the third. The team is complete.

The driver then opens the slip-rails of the yard and leads his team out to the dray. He then puts them in position in front of the dray, and backs the team until he has the two last, or pole bullocks, in their places, one on either side of the dray pole. The ring on the pole bullocks' yoke is much larger than the other rings, large enough for the end of the pole to go through it. The driver puts the pole through this ring, and drops a thick iron pin into a hole in front of the ring. Another pin is already behind it, so that the pole is now fastened to the yoke. He then removes the hook of the chain of the next bullocks from the ring on the pole bullocks' yoke, and puts it into an iron loop at the end of the pole, and the whole operation is complete.

All these movements of the bullocks are done by the word of command, and by certain motions of the whip, such as letting the lash fall gently on the off-side of the shoulder when you want to bring the bullock towards you, and pushing him quietly with the butt end of the whip when you want him to turn away from you.

Before I pass on to the year 1853 I must make another quotation from my official report, dated December 31, 1852:—" In reporting upon the state of this Institution " for the past four months, the subject which, on account " of its importance, first demands our attention is the " great extent to which sickness and mortality have " prevailed amongst the inmates during this period. But " I have the happiness of being able to state that, in two " cases of death which have lately occurred, the last hours " of the sufferers were so cheered by the peace and hope " which they derived from their belief in the blessed " truths of the Gospel, that our sorrow, we may say, " has, for the time, been turned into joy, and our " mourning into gladness. Still, these frequent deaths we " must needs feel to be a heavy affliction."

There were six deaths in 1852. Constantly in my addresses to the inmates, which, during times of affliction or anxiety, were given almost daily, evening prayer affording the needful opportunity, I put before our people the necessity of baptism as the entrance into the Christian brotherhood. But I no less earnestly and frequently dwelt upon the necessity of their taking hold sincerely and firmly of the hope set before them before coming forward for baptism. It was only by degrees that I could get them to come to the point, And so, as already stated, four passed away without making any such confession of their belief as would have justified the administration of baptism.

The first to be taken from us in 1852 was Manya, one of the original party on Boston Island, and the wife of Narrung. She was gentle and amiable, but had no force of character; and, although she had a long illness and much instruction, she failed to make up her mind to declare herself distinctly in favour of Christianity. Yorroke had been with us fifteen months; Memritten nine months. Charley was a very early inmate, having come in December, 1850. He was then quite a boy—a merry, laughing fellow, very well disposed, but wanting in ballast. But in his last illness his mind matured rapidly, and he became in heart a true, penitent and firm believer in his Lord. Before I left the station on a certain Saturday, to go into Port Lincoln for the Sunday services, I had arranged to baptize him on the Monday. Some other engagement, however, detained me, and the poor dear fellow passed away in my absence. I saw nothing in his condition on Saturday to lead me to suppose that the end was so near. I was grieved that the sacrament had been wanting to him, but he had earnestly desired it, and the omission was from no fault or backwardness on his part, and we were able to rejoice in his translation to a better world.

The next, Ullean Ullean, had been with us only eleven months. He had not been in the Adelaide school, and was wholly uninstructed. He was, however, a most willing worker, and was the first to handle the plough.

Kaituan died early in December, 1852. He had been with us nearly a year and eleven months. He had been baptized and died rejoicing, believing in his Lord with all his heart.

It was with real sorrow that I made the following state-ment in the same official Report which I have already quoted: " I regret to state that I have been compelled to " dismiss after so long a period of probation one of our " ' original members,' a man from the neighbourhood of " Lake Bonney, called Popjoy. His case, has been more " than once mentioned in my Reports. He was the only " one amongst the original members who had grown up to

E

" manhood without receiving any kind of training or in-
" struction. The experiment of civilization, as regarded
" him, was therefore different from any of the others, and
" his case was one of peculiar interest. He has been
" always extremely difficult to manage, and, on account of
" the ungovernable violence of his temper, he set a very
" mischievous example to the other inmates. Indeed, his
" paroxysms of rage were at times by no means without
" danger to those with whom he was enraged. I was
" therefore at length obliged, although most reluctantly, to
" relieve the Institution of his presence." He was a fine,
powerful man, an excellent worker, and very willing. He
and Neruid were related, Popjoy being probably some ten
years the senior. He was not baptized. The name is a
very singular one. Many years after, when a passenger in
a P. and O. steamer, I heard that there was a man of that
name also a passenger, who had been a settler somewhere
in the interior of N.S.W. The white men often call
natives by the names of their employers. Mr. Moorhouse
informed me, about eleven months after Popjoy's dismissal,
that he had died in Adelaide of consumption.

After recounting, in my official Report quoted above, our
losses by death in the year 1852, I added, " Another
" female is now so ill that it is quite evident that her end
" is approaching. She is herself quite conscious that such
" is the case, and is looking forward with peace and hope
" to the better home which she believes is prepared for her
" above." A note is added at a later date in these words:
" She died full of faith and peace and hope, January 5,
" 1853." Her name was Merari. She came to us in
June, 1851, and had been baptized in December, 1852.

1853.—I have already stated that the minds of several of
our inmates had been dwelling much on the question of
their baptism for a considerable time. Happily these
searchings of heart ripened and bore good fruit early in
1853. At the beginning of February we had the privilege
of receiving a visit from the Bishop, and when it was
known that he was coming amongst us, ten of the men
and one woman expressed their desire to be baptized by
the Bishop during his visit. The Bishop was good enough
to write an account of this visit to S.P.G. I venture to
incorporate the greater part of his letter with this my
narrative.

Whatever I then wrote about our proceedings came from me as from a worker in the midst of his occupations. The Bishop came, on the occasion which he describes, as an observer, deeply interested in the work; having helped it, and being ready to help it in every possible way. The statement of an observer's impressions must always have an interest specially its own, which no details from the worker's pen can interfere with. I omit from his letter some descriptions of the country, because I have already given them; I omit also some remarks on attempts in general to civilize aboriginal races. The Bishop tells, in his own words, what he saw and what he joined in at Poonindie.

" *Port Lincoln, Feb.* 14, 1853.

" My dear Sir,—Having long been desirous of visiting the native Mission at Poonindie, under Archdeacon M. B. Hale, to ascertain its progress, and report to the *Society* upon the degree of success with which his disinterested efforts have been blessed, I gladly avail myself of a favourable opportunity; and, embarking in a small coasting trader of fifty tons, which plies between Adelaide and this place, reached this settlement, the little township of Port Lincoln, on Thursday, Feb. 3, having left home on the preceding Monday. After officiating, together with the Archdeacon, in the church (St. Thomas's) at Port Lincoln on Sunday, Feb. 6th, when I confirmed five young women, residents of the place, we left for Poonindie early on Tuesday morning. The road winds along the picturesque shores of Boston Bay, and after crossing the pretty little valley of the river Tod, brought us to cottages and huts, which forms the Mission settlement of Poonindie. Besides the clap-boarded cottage in which the Archdeacon lives, three others accommodate the schoolmaster, the overseer, and the working foreman. Fourteen smaller huts contain eleven married native couples, and the other, children of both sexes. A kitchen and offices, washing-shed, &c., complete the present hamlet of Poonindie; at some distance above and below which, on the river, three other stone detached cottages also belong to the Mission. The " Native Reserve," set apart by the local government for the use of the Institution, comprises a fine, grassy, park-like plain, at the base of a range of hills of moderate height, which afford pasturage for between 3,000 and 4,000 sheep.

"Much has been said in proof of the impossibility of converting the natives—of two girls who, after having been employed as servants at Government House, subsequently returned to native life and habits. But what are the facts? They were not suitable wives for Europeans; if married to natives, they must needs belong to their affianced husbands, or run the risk of being *speared*. Few or no colonists would have taken them as domestic servants, unwilling to take the necessary trouble with them, or exercise the requisite patience; and thus, after a few months or years of schooling and superficial civilization, together with a little Christian knowledge, rather than a real change of heart, they were thrown back upon native life, or became the degraded victims of European vice. Their case only demonstrated the necessity of an Institution, such as the Archdeacon has succeeded in setting on foot, for the reception of the elder native children who had been partially educated at Adelaide, at the most critical period of life, when approaching manhood. He devoted himself to the holy object of converting, if possible, the remnant that was left, and saving them from the ravages of disease and infamy. The principles on which he proposed to proceed were pointed out by past experience and former failures. They were isolation, industrial education, as well as the usual schooling; marriage, separate dwellings, hiring and service for wages; gradual and progressive moral improvement based upon Christian instruction, Christian worship, and Christian superintendence. Without disturbing the school at Adelaide (which he proposed to leave as an elementary training establishment), he desired to draft, from time to time, the elder boys and girls to the Mission Station at Port Lincoln. For this purpose, Boston Island, which closes Boston Bay, Port Lincoln, to seaward, containing about four square miles, was pitched upon for the Mission. But the inability to find fresh water, after sinking several wells, necessitated removal, after a sojourn of a few weeks, to some better watered spot. Poonindie, on the river Tod, was accordingly selected; and, in order to carry out the system of isolation and industrial employment, the surrounding district was proclaimed a Native Reserve, exempting it, therefore, from sale to private individuals. The various duties of farming sheep and cattle herding for the young men offered the best means of training these young people to the habits and duties of civilized life. The Archdeacon had first to gain their confidence, and win their affection. His simple, kind, firm, Christian earnestness—teaching, controlling, reproving, governing, in short, with enlightened charity, these children of the bush—has at length been blessed with a considerable degree of success. Many young adult natives, who would have belonged to the most degraded portion of the human family, are now clothed and in their right minds, sitting at the feet of Jesus, and intelligently worshipping, through Him, their heavenly Father.

"The Mission now consists of fifty-four natives, comprising eleven married couples; the rest children of either sex, thirteen being from the Port Lincoln district. The married couples have each their little hut, built of the trunks of the shea-oak set up in the ground, the interstices being neatly plastered and whitewashed, roofed with broad paling. The other children in small divisions occupy the remaining ones. They have their meals in common in the general kitchen; the working party first, then the women and children. Narrung, one of the elder young men, assisted by two mates, is steward, butcher, and cook. At half-past six in the morning, and in the evening, after sun-down, all assemble at the Archdeacon's cottage, for the reading of Scripture and prayer. The Schoolmaster leads the singing of a simple hymn, and the low, soft voices of the natives make pleasing melody. A plain exposition follows. After breakfast they go to their several employments: the cowherds milk, &c.; some were engaged in putting up posts and rails for a stock-yard; the shepherds were with their flocks; two assisted the bricklayer, one preparing mortar, the other laying bricks. At the proper season they plow, reap, shear, make bricks, burn charcoal, cut wood; do, in fact, under the direction of the overseer, the usual work of a station. Six hours are the limits of the working day; they are unequal to more. Shepherds and first-class labourers receive 8s. per week and rations; second-class, 5s.; third, 3s. 6d.; fourth, 2s. 6d. The younger children attend school; the married women wash, and learn sewing clothes, making and mending. Such is an outline of the occupation, education, and religious training adopted at Poonindie.

which, begun with very limited means, and with no previous instance of success to encourage hope, has nevertheless, through a blessing upon the Archdeacon's patient, untiring, quiet zeal, reached a very promising state of maturity. Thus far the Institution is an exception to the list of Australian Missionary failures.

" Let us look at the present results, under the heads of Civilization, Moral Training, and Christian Attainment.

"Firstly. We find eleven married couples decently clothed, clean in their persons, keeping their own huts and clothes in order, and much attached to each other—in the place of the promiscuous unchastity, and the brutal degradation of the native women in their wild state. A farm of twenty acres has been fenced, plowed, reaped, and stacked, by these children of the soil ; two flocks are wholly under their charge. These they have shorn, besides two other flocks belonging to settlers ; and five were just about to shear the lambs of Mr. Peter, at eighteen shillings per hundred. I saw an excellent kiln of bricks which, under the direction of a brickmaker from Adelaide, they had helped to make, mould, and burn. In fact, while the other settlers at Port Lincoln were much hampered by the migration of their servants and shepherds to the Victoria Diggings, the Archdeacon was able to carry on the improvement of the Mission premises, the labours at the farm, as well as assist his neighbours with native shearers, who shear remarkably well.

"Secondly. In regard to Moral Training, the wild native knows little or nothing of the value of money or property ; but at Poonindie the Mission lads earn weekly wages, and, what is more, " shop " for themselves at the store in Port Lincoln, or even send up orders to Adelaide for goods. This indicates a real mental and moral development. The following purchases were made by one of the Mission natives, Kewrie, for himself and friend, while I was present : a pair of shoes, two pairs of trowsers, a blue woollen shirt, a packet of currants and raisins for puddings, a flask of salad oil for the hair ; a bonnet was looked at for his wife, but left for her determination, and a shawl for the throat rejected as being too dear. The same youth, had he been left to native influences upon leaving school, would probably have become, after a short time, a dirty, ragged, diseased, lazy sheep-stealer, or an occasional hewer of wood and drawer of water for some of the inhabitants of Adelaide, or settlers in the Bush. He is now a nice-looking, decent, intelligent, well-conducted young man.

"Thirdly. With respect to conversion. When the Archdeacon came in from Poonindie to meet me, he was followed by ten of the elder boys and young men, who asked leave to go and meet the Bishop. Some I had known in the Sunday School at Adelaide. I was agreeably surprised to see them nicely dressed in the usual clothing worn by settlers; check shirts, light summer coats, plaid trowsers, with shoes and felt hats— articles mostly purchased with their own earnings. They were better dressed than the labouring class in general at home. They had brought their blankets, blacking, brushes, &c., making the broad verandah of a wood-shed their sleeping place, and cooking their meals at a fire in the yard. Not far off was a small native camp, and the contrast between these two groups would have convinced any candid observer of the truth for which the Archdeacon has always contended, viz., that the aborigines are not only entitled to our Christian regard, but are capable, under God's blessing, of being brought out of darkness into light, and from the power of Satan unto God.

"It was very pleasing to see these young men, on Sunday morning before church, sitting together reading in their Testaments or hymn-books, which they had brought with them, and afterwards filling, at both services, two benches in the pretty little church. Most of them were Catechumens, whom the Archdeacon thought he could recommend as fit to be baptized. Accordingly, on Thursday, the 10th, at Poonindie, I conversed severally with ten men, and Tanda, the wife of Conwillan, in the presence of the Archdeacon. The native manner is naturally shy, reserved, and incommunicative, but gentle and unimpassioned. After hearing them, and asking them questions, I agreed with the Archdeacon that there was good ground for admitting them by baptism into the ark of Christ's Church, believing them to be subjects of God's grace and favour. We held regular evening service at sundown; and after the second lesson I baptized Thomas Nytchie, James Narrung, Samuel Conwillan, Joseph Mudlong, David Tolbonko, John Wangaru, Daniel Toodko, Matthew Kewrie, Timothy Tartan, Isaac Pitpowie, and Martha Tanda, wife of Conwillan. The other women and girls are not yet so advanced as Martha and Annette, a little Swan River native, who has long formed part of the Archdeacon's family. Each native answered for himself distinctly, according to the service for Adult Baptism, and, from their devotional manner and previous answers, I have reason to believe that they understood and intended to keep the vow which they then voluntarily made. On the following morning I consecrated the cemetery, where the remains of those who have died repose. Of these, eight in number, *three*, in addition to Takanarro (of whose last illness and happy death I sent you a printed account), gave strong evidence of their dying in faith and assured hope.

" I must here observe, with respect to this mortality, that compared with Europeans, the ordinary native is slight in frame and feeble in constitution, easily brought low by sickness, and pining away often from unaccountable causes, principally pulmonary complaints, aggravated by their own thoughtlessness and roving mode of life. The seeds of disease have also been widely spread through the native tribes since their contact with Europeans : and hence the dwindling away of the race from premature death and fruitless marriage.

" One more incident I may mention in proof of their progress in civilization : a cricket match played by the Poonindie lads and young men, on a holiday given on the occasion of my visit. I was pleased at watching, with the Archdeacon, two Australian native 'elevens' thus enjoying themselves, and remarked, not only their neatness in ' fielding and batting,' but, what was far more worthy of note, the perfect good humour which prevailed throughout the games ; no ill-temper shown, or angry appeals to the umpire, as is generally the case in a match of *Whites*.

" I have little more to add, than that the Mission is again strengthened by the accession of Mr. George Wollaston, son of Archdeacon Wollaston, who will act as overseer of the sheep and farm labour. A good schoolmistress is shortly expected from England, and thus the education of the younger boys and girls will be well carried on. A new school-room is projected, and subscriptions are collecting for the purpose. It appears to me that the Mission is so consolidated as to admit of gradual enlargement. There is now a small body of trained Christian natives, the nucleus of the native Church. The Archdeacon, and all friends of Missions, have reason to thank God and take courage. His blessing will never fail to attend enlightened zeal, chastened and sustained as that is, in Mr. Hale, by Christian love and firmness of purpose.

"I sail in a few days for Adelaide when the wind serves.
"Yours truly,
"Rev. E. Hawkins.   "Augustus Adelaide."

"P.S.—We set sail on Saturday, the 19th, and reached Adelaide on Monday morning, after a quick passage."

I have more than once stated that the question of baptism had been for some time gradually and steadily working in the thoughts of some of the men, and, as I hoped and believed, ripening their minds for a decided declaration of their faith. That all-important event, the first public baptism, had now taken place. The leader in the movement had undoubtedly been Narrung, and he had been cordially supported by his younger brother, who had been more steady in his attendance at the Adelaide school, and was a very good scholar. Narrung, as he confessed, had neglected the school. He learned to read at Poonindie, and, by going over the same ground very many times, he could at length make his way through two or three chapters of St. John's Gospel. The seventeenth chapter was the one he especially delighted to spell over.

I find in my diary an entry headed as follows:—"Sup-"plemental entry to diary, July 17th, 1852. There has "been about Narrung ever since he has been with us, a "sweetness and amiableness of disposition, a docility of "mind, and a propriety of life and conversation which have "made him a universal favourite. And of late, I am most "thankful to say, I have seen reason to believe that his "naturally good disposition has, under God's grace, "ripened into a really serious and religious state of "mind. He was one of the original party which was sent "to Port Lincoln by Mr. Moorhouse, just at this time "about two years ago. He and his partner Manya, were "assigned to Captain Bishop, in whose service they made "themselves very useful during the interval which elapsed

" between their arrival in the settlement and their going
" with me to Boston Island. He always treated Manya
" with kindness, but I think they had lived together for
" nearly twelve months before they manifested anything
" like a real attachment towards each other. They became
" at length very much attached, and on the 17th of October,
" 1851, I duly and regularly solemnized their marriage,
" together with that of another original couple, Konwillan
" and Tanda.

" Shortly after this, Manya, with three other of our
" native girls, went on a visit to Adelaide. She was ill the
" greater part of the time she was there. And, after her
" return she was for some time alarmingly ill at our house at
" Port Lincoln. After a time, however, she got very much
" better, and joined Narrung and her other companions at
" Poonindie. Narrung's affection for her displayed itself
" in a very striking manner during this illness; so much so,
" that at the annual meeting of the South Australian Church
" Society at Adelaide, I made mention of some incidents
" illustrating his affection for her, and his anxiety about
" her health.

" When her death occurred " [after an illness subse-
quent to the one recorded above] " he was most deeply
" affected, and took it much to heart. And I have this
" further ground for believing that it was to him a real afflic-
" tion, viz., that it appears to have produced in him the best
" fruit of affliction, and his religious feelings have evidently
" assumed a deeper and more decided character since that
" event.

" I made great efforts to bring about this result of deepen-
" ing the religious feeling, both as regards Narrung and
" also the rest of the natives, and I strove for it both by
" general exhortations to them all and also by means of
" private conversations. Narrung responded to my efforts
" in a way that gave me the deepest gratification and moved
" me to my inmost soul with thankfulness to my merciful,
" gracious God for His goodness in this and in all other ways so
" abundantly evidenced. Of late Narrung has moved down
" here again from Colombo (a hut and sheep station on
" Mount Gawler), and forms one of a party of four or five of
" the elder and more trustworthy and intelligent single men,
" who have their quarters at one of the stone cottages.

" And now I arrive at last at the conversation which I

" had with him this evening, whilst he was sitting with me
" in my hut, I said, ' Narrung, I hope you boys down at
" that place (the stone cottages were a little way off the
" village) talk about good things, and do not spend all your
" time in foolish talk.' He said, ' Oh yes, we talk about
" good things. That day when I came down from Colombo
" (meaning the day he came down for his wife's funeral),
" then I said to them boys, " Now we must think about good
" things. We must talk about what we do, not to do
" wicked things."' I said ' And you always pray down there ' ?
" ' Oh, yes, we pray ; only one night we forgot, then we said
" the next night, ' We forgot to pray last night, we must
" not forget to pray.' I asked who it was who said that,
" then he said, ' I said that to them.' Then I asked, ' And
" when you said that, were they all ready to pray and liked
" to say prayers ? ' ' Oh yes, then we knelt down, and
" Toodko (his younger brother before referred to) said
" prayers and we repeated after him.' In the course of the
" conversation he said, ' We must pray to God to forgive
" us all them wicked things and mischief what we have done.
" I often say this to boys, We must pray to God to forgive
" us.' And then he said, with every indication of manner
" and voice of deep and sincere feeling, ' I pray God to
" forgive me ; I hope God forgive me. I hope I never do
" them things again which I have done wrong.' Again in the
" course of the conversation, I said something about the ad-
" vantage of being able to attend the morning and evening
" prayers. He said, ' When I was in the Bush shepherding
" there, I say to myself I shall ask Mr. Hale to let me go
" down to Poonindie and stop there, then I can always go
" to prayers with the other boys and hear about good
" things.'

" He then again told me, as he has several times told me
" before, how constantly his thoughts were upon good things
" when he is out in the Bush shepherding. ' All day I
" think about good things. We must try not to do wicked
" things. We must pray to God, and try to please
" Him.' About his baptism we, of course, always talk
" upon the occasion of such conversations as the present
" one. I do not wish to urge him on to it alone, as he has
" a little feeling of shrinking from being the first to take
" this step by himself. And I have great hope that it will be
" the gracious pleasure of my merciful God to suffer me to

" see, before any long time, others coming forward also, and
" bearing Narrung company in his holy desires and wishes."

The hope thus devoutly expressed on July 17, 1852,
was, through the great goodness and mercy of God,
abundantly realized within a period of six months from that
time when Narrung, not alone, but accompanied by no less
than ten of his companions, received the blessed sacrament
of baptism at the hands of the Bishop of the Diocese.

These details of my conversations with Narrung may
serve to illustrate the manner in which the question of
baptism had been steadily coming to the front in the
minds of some of our inmates. I thought I could not
illustrate the movement better than by connecting this
quiet progress in Narrung's mind immediately with the
account of the Bishop's visit and the celebration of
baptism. I must now, however, go back to the first day
of the year 1853. On that day a most important change
took place in my position in relation to the South Australian
Government. The documents here introduced will, to a
certain extent, explain the nature of that change; but I
shall feel it necessary to give, presently, further explanation,
that the reader may be enabled to understand some of our
surrounding circumstances.

With respect to the documents, they were, of course,
published for general information at the time to which they
belonged. But, in compliance with my particular request,
they were again published in connection with my last
returns when I was leaving Port Lincoln in 1856. They
are as follows :—

" PORT LINCOLN, 20*th Sept.*, 1852.
" MAY IT PLEASE YOUR EXCELLENCY,—

" In approaching your Excellency with this petition for
an increase in the amount of the funds placed at my disposal for promoting the welfare of the aboriginal natives of
this Province, I beg respectfully to solicit your Excellency's
attention to the following circumstances :—

" That the Native Training Institution, which I formed
by means of funds granted to me for that purpose, and
which has now been in active operation for a period of two
years, has been blessed with a remarkable amount of
success, and is steadily accomplishing the purposes for
which it was established.

" That this success has itself led to a very large increase

in the number of inmates (the number being at the present time 45), and that the expenses attendant upon its support have also been very greatly increased.

" That the rise in the price of provisions has affected us to a very serious extent, and advantage has been taken of the unsettled state of affairs by the owner of the coasting vessel which visits this port to make most exorbitant charges for freight.

" As touching generally the subject of the expenditure of money upon the natives, all experience has tended to show that considerable sums of money *must* be expended upon them in one way or other, and no one can for a moment question that measures for their permanent improvement and the amelioration of their condition are infinitely better than coercion and punishment.

" I enclose herewith a formal proposition to undertake the support and carrying on of the existing Institution, and also of the school for the children of the aboriginal natives of this district under a certain contract, and I enclose also a certificate from the Government Resident of the district having reference to the said contract.

" My reasons for wishing to enter upon the undertaking as a contractor are these :—

" 1. To obtain liberty of action with respect to the funds which is absolutely necessary to enable me to make the most of my means. In carrying on farming and other operations upon rather an extensive scale, in order to afford occupation to the natives, and make the Institution, as far as possible, self-supporting, I should be often obliged to make sales and purchases which it would be difficult to bring in satisfactorily into statements of accounts submitted in detail to the Government.

" 2. Even supposing that my accounts were likely to be of the plainest and most simple character, the amazing inconvenience to which we are subjected in this place by reason of the irregularity of the communication with Adelaide, would make it almost impracticable for me to render in my accounts at the proper times, and in a correct and satisfactory manner.

" To guard, as far as may be, against any misconception with respect to my object in entering into the matter as a contractor, and as an apology for myself, being a person in Holy Orders, entering into a contract at all, I have thought fit to attach to my propositions for the contract a solemn declaration as to the motives by which I am actuated in this transaction, and declaring that I am in no way influenced by the desire to make a gain or profit by the undertaking.

"I remain,

"Your Excellency's obliged and faithful servant,

"MATHEW B. HALE.

"His Excellency Sir H. E. F. YOUNG."

"I, Mathew Blagden Hale, being a person in Holy Orders, and being desirous of entering into a contract under the Government of this Province of South Australia for the performance of certain duties for the benefit of the aboriginal natives, consider it to be due to my sacred calling to make the following solemn declaration touching the motives by which I am actuated in desiring to undertake the said duties and to enter into a contract for their performance.

"I, Matthew Blagden Hale, do solemnly declare before Almighty God, that I am moved to this work by feelings of pity and compassion towards that unhappy race, whose welfare those works are intended to promote; and because I believe from my heart that I cannot in any other way so effectually promote the glory of God, or make Him an acceptable offering as by devoting myself to the unwearied performance of these works of mercy.

"And I do further solemnly declare that I have no wish or desire to make any gain or profit by the said contract, or in any way to derive from it any pecuniary benefit or advantage; but that I wish to undertake these duties as a contract, simply as matter of convenience, and because I shall be thereby enabled to employ the funds at my disposal to the greatest advantage for promoting the proposed objects.

"I, Mathew Blagden Hale, undertake to support and carry on the Natives' Training Institution now under my care, the future and duties of which (it having been established for a period of two years) are by past and present practices sufficiently marked out and defined; and I undertake to receive into the said Institution, in addition to the present inmates, any person, of whatever age or sex, and whether half-castes or wholly of the aboriginal race, as shall be sent to me by the Protector of Aborigines. And I undertake also to relieve the Government of all expenses connected with the school for the children of aboriginal natives of this district, at present under the care of Mr. Schürmann, and to use all diligence to draw to the said school, and to retain in it, as many native children as pos-sible, and to feed, clothe, and educate them, and to endeavour to train them to the performance of works of industry, and in the habits of civilised life ; and to impart to them, so far as they shall be able to receive it, a know-ledge of the way of salvation, through our blessed Lord and Saviour Jesus Christ.

" These duties I undertake to perform for the sum of £1,000 (one thousand pounds) per annum, the said sum to be paid to me, or my order, by the Colonial Treasurer, in monthly instalments, so long as I shall continue to furnish to His Excellency, the Lieut.-Governor, and the Executive Council, good and sufficient evidence (the nature of such evidence to be determined by themselves) that the above-named duties are being actually and faithfully performed. And I desire that this contract should begin to take effect on and after the 1st day of January, 1853.

"(*Signed*) MATHEW BLAGDEN HALE."

" GOVERNMENT RESIDENCY, PORT LINCOLN,
"*Sept.* 20*th*, 1852.

" Being well aware of the objects which were con-templated in the formation of the Natives' Training Institution in this place under Archdeacon Hale, and having had frequent opportunities of seeing and observing the progress of the said Institution since the period of its first formation, now two years ago ; I hereby give it as my opinion, that the experiment so made has been successful in its results, and that the purposes for which it was established are in course of being gradually and steadily obtained.

" I have also read and considered the terms of the contract which Archdeacon Hale wishes to enter into for the future support and carrying on the school for the children of aboriginal parents of this district, at present under the care of Mr. Schürmann. And I hereby give it as my opinion, that the sum of £1,000 per annum is not more than sufficient to enable Archdeacon Hale to fulfil

that contract, and to carry out, in an efficient and satisfactory manner, the combined purposes of the said Institution and the said school.

"*(Signed)* CHAS. DRIVER, J.P.,
"*Government Resident.*"

COLONIAL SECRETARY'S OFFICE, ADELAIDE,
Oct. 13*th*, 1852.

"SIR,—I have the honour to inform you, that the
Lieutenant-Governor approves of your offer to carry out
certain objects with regard to the natives at Port Lincoln,
for the annual sum of £1,000, to be paid, on your order, by
the Colonial Treasurer, in monthly instalments, so long as
His Excellency shall be satisfied that the duties, in respect
of which this payment is to be made, are faithfully fulfilled.

" The conditions embraced in this arrangement are :—

" 1st.   That commencing on the 1st January, 1853, you
shall support and carry on the Native Training Institution
now under your care, the nature and duties of which are,
by past and present practice, sufficiently marked out and
defined ; and that you will receive into the said Institution,
in addition to the present inmates, any person of whatever
age or sex, and whether half-castes or wholly of the aboriginal
·race, who may be sent to you by the Protector of Aborigines.

" 2nd.   That you relieve the Government of all expenses
connected with the school for the children of aboriginal
parents in the Port Lincoln district, at present under the
care of Mr. Schürmann, and that you use all diligence to
draw to the said school, and to retain in it, as many of these
native children as possible; and that you feed, clothe, and
educate them, endeavouring to train them to the performance of works of industry, and in the habits of civilized
life, and to impart to them, so far as they shall be able to
receive it, a knowledge of the truths of the Christian
religion.

" I have, &c.,
"(Signed,)   B. T. FINNIS,
"*Colonial Secretary.*
" To the Very Rev. Archdeacon Hale."

I must now explain that the natives of the neighbourhood of Port Lincoln, with whom I was from that time to
be brought into close contact, by receiving their children from

Mr. Schürmann's school, differed, in some very important particulars, from the tribes from which our first inmates had sprung. Their language was quite different, and they differed in many of their customs or habits. Our first inmates came from the neighbourhood of the Murray River, which is from 1,000 to 1,500 miles more to the east than Port Lincoln. In fact it was impossible to avoid the conclusion that the two people in question had come upon the Continent at opposite points : one on the East Coast and the other on the West.

The most important difference, bearing upon their civilization, relates to, what I suppose I must call, their marriage customs. Amongst the Murray natives, a middle-aged man claims a right to certain female children. They are said to have fallen in some mysterious way to him as his lawful property, and when he thinks fit he takes them to be his wives and servants ; and one sees a big, burly man, whose features are almost hidden by the profusion of hair on his head and face, stalking along at his ease, and two, or perhaps three, miserable looking little females toiling after him, carrying all the family possessions.

Young men are not allowed to have wives—the girls of their own age having been appropriated, even in childhood, by men old enough to be their fathers. Such a custom as this must necessarily have a most demoralizing effect upon any people amongst whom it prevails, and must also be a terrible hindrance in the way of efforts made for their civilization. The Port Lincoln natives have no such custom as this. There were pleasing instances of man and wife having lived together from youth to old age, with offspring of various ages around them. The Adelaide school suffered grievously from the interference of the elders with the children. There was no such interference on the part of the Port Lincoln natives when I took in hand to deal with their children. When the children were troublesome and ran away for a few days to visit some old haunts or old friends in the Bush, it was their own doing. Some had absented themselves from Mr. Schürmann's school at the time that I took charge of his children. But I believe all the absentees afterwards joined their schoolmates at Poonindie.

The district of Port Lincoln (using that phrase in a very wide sense) had, about the time of our going there, acquired

F

a sad notoriety on account of the number of murders committed by natives upon white men. These murders were all of the same kind, the unfortunate victims being solitary individuals, in charge either of sheep on the run or of a shepherd's hut. The object in all cases was the acquisition of food—either sheep to be driven away from the flocks and afterwards killed and eaten, or flour and sugar and tobacco to be found in the hut and carried off.

But none of the outrages occurred near the township of Port Lincoln, and, therefore, not near Poonindie. The natives about us were a perfectly quiet and harmless set of people. There was excellent fishing at various places along the coast. They had different methods of fishing; the usual method was to spear the fish in the water, and it was astonishing to what skill and accuracy of aim some of them attained.

Although I frequently employed them to do odd jobs, they, of course, stood upon a totally different footing from the inmates of the Institution. All those who were enrolled as inmates had to conform strictly to the habits of civilized life. They had all to be in their own proper sleeping places at night; they had to attend prayers in the house, take their breakfast, dinner, &c., at the proper time, and attend prayers again at night—over the outside, or Wurley natives—Wurley was the name of the little temporary habitations which they set up for themselves, made of the branches of trees, reeds, rushes, &c.—I did not attempt to exercise any control; and when I employed them it was always by the job, not by the day.

The jobs at which they were employed might be clearing a given piece of ground of stumps of trees, roots, &c., or cutting down the trees on a certain space, or making rough fences by cutting down and putting together trees or branches. This was quite a sufficient fence for sheep; but the small branches soon became dry and brittle, and the fences required frequent watching and frequent repairing. The payment to the Wurley natives would be certain specified rations per day, *i.e.*, so much flour, sugar, tea and tobacco, and a small money payment. If a good many hands, say ten or twelve, were put on upon a job, then one of the older men amongst the inmates would be set over them to see that the work was properly done. But a small party of the more trust-worthy or skilful men would do the appointed work quite satisfactorily without any superintendence.

They had, of course, frequent opportunities of seeing the superior comfort in which our people lived. But I never could discover that anyone had, at any time, the slightest ambition to be enrolled as an inmate. Neither could we induce anyone ever to listen seriously to our instruction. The trial was repeatedly made, not only by myself and the other white people of the Institution, but by some of our natives. Toodko especially manifested the greatest desire to impart to them some knowledge of Christianity. But all in vain. The man to whom he was talking would look at him with a good-humoured expression on his face, probably smiling internally at this kind solicitude, but one would look in vain for any sign of even the smallest spark of interest in what was being said, or any indication that the man was trying to, or wished to, understand it. Then again these people had the case of their own children before them, *i.e.*, those who had been brought up in Mr. Schürmann's school; they saw their children growing up, and being taught in the Christian faith, their conduct influenced and ruled thereby. But nothing made any impression upon them.

It would appear, then, that our Poonindie experience proved two things :—

(1). That, in the case of an Australian aborigine, if he is put under instruction when he is quite young; if his intellect is kept growing and his mind expanding, that growth and expansion may be continued in after years; that if the truths of Christianity are fittingly put before him his natural simplicity of mind and his docility will dispose him readily to receive those truths, and that he may, by the grace of God, become not only a Christian, but a Christian of a high stamp and a truly spiritually-minded person; such, I say unhesitatingly, were Narrung, Toodko, and Mudlong amongst our inmates.

(2). What we learn, secondly, at any rate what I feel that I learned from my long intercourse with some of the amiable well-disposed Port Lincoln natives, is that if the intellect is not stimulated in early years, not cultivated, nothing set before the mind to help it on in expansion and growth, it becomes hopelessly dwarfed or stunted. There is a time for growth and expansion. But if that time is lost it can never be recovered.

I have already dwelt at some length upon the case of Neruid. I suppose him to have been about seventeen or eighteen when he came into our hands. His mind was operated upon by a very powerful motive. He had an intense desire to become a Poonindie native. But even at the age I have named the time for growth of mind or intellect was apparently rapidly passing away with him. Although he was very anxious to learn, he could not make much progress. He could not at all keep pace with the children. But by God's grace the efforts which his strong will enabled him to make were sufficient to open his mind to receive the truths of Christianity. He received those truths in the love of them. He lived the life of a Christian for twenty years; and when he died his friends gladly testified concerning him that he had left them "a good example." But his case was a solitary one. No case like it was ever brought to my knowledge. That which I have now stated is the lesson which I learned from my intercourse with the aborigines of the Port Lincoln district. But I learned a very similar lesson from my intercourse with the peasantry of our Western Counties of England fifty years ago.

I suppose, as a result of the very great efforts which have been made in promoting public education during the last twenty-five or thirty years, there are comparatively few persons now who have not attended schools in their early years. But at the time I speak of the number of persons amongst the peasants who could not read was very large, and one almost never heard of a person who had learned to read after he or she had grown to man's or woman's estate. I am far from saying that this ignorance or indisposition to mental effort formed any difficulty in the way of these people receiving the truths of Christianity. I know that that was not the case, because, as a rule, they had been hearing about these truths, in one way or another, almost from their infancy. What I mean to say is this: that it would appear that, in the case of persons whose intellects have not been aroused or quickened by ordinary school instruction in early life, a certain measure of torpidity creeps over their minds, which seems to deaden any desire for instruction, and stands in the way of their even learning to read in after life, though they must know quite well that, for very many reasons, it would be greatly to their advantage to do so. But to return to the question of the natives. Although they have been rapidly dying out in the settled districts, there are still thousands of square miles on the Australian Continent where Europeans have not settled, and where the natives still remain in force : and there is in the minds of very many persons an earnest desire to do something towards civilising and Christianising some members at least of this unhappy race. If it please God to permit me to accomplish what I have in view, I will add to my narrative a separate paper describing my views of the way in which I think the work should be gone about. I will now only say this, that the object to be primarily aimed at in all cases should be the getting hold of and instructing the children. The children of this race quickly spring up to maturity.

Let me give an instance. Mr. Schürmann commenced his school a few months before I commenced at Poonindie. In two-years-and-a-half from the time he commenced he had three girls well taught, and so far grown up that they had become restless and unsettled at the school : and he feared that they might be enticed back into the Bush to live again with the Wurley natives. Knowing that we had at Poonindie many more young men than young women, he begged of me to see if I could not arrange for these three girls to join the Institution as wives of three of our young men. The arrangement was brought about.

The girls came to us. They proved to be suitable inmates, and in the course of time, gave satisfactory evidence of an earnest desire to lead Christian lives, and were baptized. Surely, then, Mr. Schürmann's school was not long in bearing fruit. Any one devoting himself to missionary work may well be prepared to wait three or four years, and at the end of that period his pupils may have become well grounded in the facts and truths of Ch

in call attention to the fact that the two eaching the children and trying to teach the our case being tried simultaneously, the Lincoln being the subjects of our experi- hat were the results ? As regards the children, in the course of about four or five years after Mr. Schürmann opened his school, we had in the Poonindie Institution several of his pupils as members of a Christian community, some as baptized Christians, others as Catechumens preparing for baptism. As regards the adults, during the same space of time we had failed to make a single convert. It is true that some of the men would, in the most patient and good-humoured manner listen to us, so far as the hearing of the ear went ; but we had failed to perceive the slightest indication that a single individual took the least interest in what we were saying, or felt any desire whatever to understand the matter.

Having so often repeated Mr. Schürmann's name I think I ought to say something more about him. He, and some other Lutheran pastors, were sent out by some German missionary society to labour, in any way they could, amongst the Australian aborigines, and, in the year 1849, Mr. Schürmann, under the authority of the Government, started the school for native children on a spot about half-way between Port Lincoln and the then Poonindie sheep station. He had a small salary as schoolmaster, and he had also a small salary as interpreter of the native language. But when the gold fever set in, and people were running away from South Australia by thousands to go to the diggings, there ensued a sort of panic—an idea that the Colony might be almost on the brink of ruin. Then there came a day, afterwards known as " Black Thursday," when a great number of Government officials were told that their services would no longer be required. Amongst the sufferers was Mr. Schürmann, who lost his interpreter-ship. He soon afterwards made up his mind to give up the school ; and it became attached to Poonindie.

It will be remembered that, in the first instance, I had nothing to do with any other natives except those who had come, or were to come, from the Adelaide school. In giving my explanation of the way in which I was brought into close contact with the Port Lincoln natives, I have been led into this digression. I now return to other matters.

The Bishop, in his letter to S. G. P. above quoted, mentions the return of Mr. Wollaston to Poonindie. It wil' remembered that he left in March, 1852, in order to jo' brother at the diggings. We were very glad of his return; especially as Mr. Minchin had, in the meantime, received an appointment from the Government as Protector of Aborigines somewhere near the head of Spencer's Gulf, and had gone to enter upon his duties.

I regret that, for the purpose of carrying on my narrative, I cannot make extracts from a diary for 1853. For I find that I have none for that year. It appears that I altogether neglected it. But, as I have already pretty fully described the various duties of the Institution, and how those duties were carried on, the loss is, perhaps, not a very serious one: more especially as I have copies of some of my official Reports to the Government.

Apparently, I had some fear that the members of the Government might be discouraged by the frequent deaths amongst us—and might be tempted to think that, even supposing that the Institution was making Christians of the inmates, this would not be of much use if they were to die immediately after. At any rate I appear to have indirectly combated any idea of that kind. In one Report " I said the spiritual advancement of the inmates has " always been the great object of my solicitude. Indeed it " is *the object* which I have in view in entering upon and " continuing to carry on the undertaking which I have in " hand. . . . The test which has been applied to the " religious principles of our little community has been of " the most severe and searching description in the great " prevalence of sickness and death. And the faith in " Christ of these poor children of the desert has been " proved to be of no false or hollow character. In the " minds of the dying it has shone more brightly and clearly " as death approached. In the minds of the living it has " remained firm and steadfast whilst the hand of death has " been busy amongst their companions."

In another Report I mentioned the death of another dear lad, Tartan. He was only a boy when he came to us at the time of our settling at Poonindie, October, 1850. He had been constant in his attendance at the Adelaide School, and was really a very good scholar, and such a cheerful, amiable fellow that every one was fond of him. He was one of the eleven baptized by the Bishop, February 10, 1853, and he was carried off by a rapid consumption on the 27th of the following month, the day being Easter Sunday.

I reported the matter to the Government in the following words :—" He was taken from us on Easter Sunday, March " 27. But, whilst we deeply deplore his loss from amongst " us, the circumstances connected with his departure were " such as to afford us the most abundant comfort and con- " solation. His latter end, as that of three of his com- " panions who had gone before him, was cheered by " his firm faith in his Blessed Redeemer, and by the joyful " hope of a blessed and glorious resurrection to eternal " life."

In yet another Report, during this same year, 1853, I wrote thus :—" I do not pretend to deny that I feel at times " greatly depressed by these afflicting dispensations. And " yet, when I consider them in all their bearings, I find no " difficulty in discerning how, in the hands of an omni- " potent and all-merciful God, these afflictions become the " instruments by which the highest and most important " purposes are worked out. There can be doubt but that " the very general serious and anxious attention which is " now paid by the natives to all matters of a religious " nature must be regarded as, in a great measure, the effect " of these frequent visitations."

It had been my constant endeavour to get this great truth firmly implanted in their minds, viz., that the great purpose for which we are placed in this world is, not merely that we may live long lives, but that we may so live as to be constantly preparing for a better life, and that if, by God's grace, we do so prepare, we should look forward to that better life cheerfully and joyfully, and gladly receive the summons to go to it when it should please God to call us. And most thankful I am to be able to say that this was the prevailing feeling in the minds of many of our inmates while still in health. It might be supposed that, under the circumstances above described, our little community would have been oppressed by a general feeling of gloom or despondency. Nothing of the sort took place. We sorrowed, truly and sincerely, for the loss of the companion- ship of our dear friends, as they were taken from us. But we sorrowed not as them that are without hope. We willingly resigned our friends to their loving Father who had taken them, knowing that our loss was their ever- lasting gain.

I must now say something about the work of the Institu-

tion. In my report for June, 1853, I wrote as follows:—
"As the different seasons come round for the performance
"of the various operations of farming the land and getting
"the land into cultivation, they serve to mark the progress
"which the natives are making in skill and general use-
"fulness. We have just now completed the ploughing
"and sowing for the present season. And the manner in
"which this has been accomplished affords the clearest
"evidence of advancement from year to year. In 1851 the
"ploughing was performed entirely by Europeans." [It
was in fact done by Mr. Wollaston.] "In 1852 it was
"performed by the natives. But I was myself constantly
"on the spot, and superintending and directing, and mark-
"ing off the lands."

"This year, superintendence and assistance from Mr.
"Wollaston at the *commencement* of the season, and to a
"*limited extent*, have been found sufficient. Upon divers
"occasions the ploughmen have gone on with their work,
"marking off the lands, and going through the whole
"process of the ploughing without even the presence of
"an European in the field for days together. In the case
"of one small paddock of about four acres, they were
"left to complete the sowing and harrowing by themselves
"without any assistance. The extent of land which has
"been thus got under crop is about twenty acres. The
"whole of it is sown with wheat."

In my report for September, I stated that another
public baptism had taken place, the date thereof was
August 6. After referring to the baptisms celebrated
by the Bishop on February 10, I go on to say:—"I
"have now the further happiness of stating that, since
"that time, I have had the privilege of baptizing sixteen
"more. Nearly the whole of these candidates last named
"belonged to that party of lads and boys whom I brought
"with me from the natives' school in Adelaide, after the
"happy death of the youth Takenarro, which occurred at
"that school in January, 1852.

"On account of the number brought to Poonindie upon
"that occasion, and on account of their being just at the
"age when youths are considered to be most impatient of
"control, I had great misgivings with respect to the evils
"which I thought might probably result from my receiving
"them at that time into the Institution. I am most

"thankful to say that my fears with respect to their
"conduct have not been by any means realized. And
"when I now find myself surrounded by these same indi-
"viduals, most of them having, by this time, sprung up
"to manhood, and when I feel that I can look upon the
"majority of them as serious and consistent Christians,
"my mind is filled with gratitude to the Almighty
"Disposer of events that I was induced to attend to the
"entreaties of these simple-hearted creatures, and to
"bring them with me upon that occasion to join their
"former companions at this place."

I then proceeded to mention how the work of God had
been helped on by the pious efforts of some of the natives
themselves: I said, "Another thing which makes this
"general attention to the things of God still more deeply
"interesting is the way in which the good work has been
"promoted and helped forward by some of the more
"influential of the young men themselves. The pious
"efforts of two of these in particular" [they were Narrung
and his brother Toodko] "have been productive of much
"good and have been attended with most beneficial
"results."

I have already stated that the Poonindie shearers, after
shearing our own sheep, took jobs of shearing at other
stations. This became quite an established yearly custom,
an arrangement which was both useful to the district and
profitable to our men. As the shearing time of 1853
approached, it occurred to me that I might contrive some
mechanical arrangement for pressing the wool into the wool
bales. The wool bale is hung inside a wooden box, the bale
and box both being open at the top, and, as the fleeces are
put in, they require, of course, to be pressed down. If this
is done without mechanical power a man stands upon the
wool, treading it down in the centre, and tucking it down
with a spade at the sides of the bale.

But this is necessarily a slow process, and, when the
elasticity of wool is taken into account, it will be at once
perceived that a very much smaller quantity of wool could
be put into a bale in this way than could be put by means
of mechanical pressure. Ships' freights are charged by
measurement, and it is therefore so much money in the
wool grower's pocket if he can reduce the number of his
bales without reducing the quantity of wool transmitted.

Very efficient wool presses are imported into the Colonies, and they are used at all large and important stations. But with our small number of sheep, one of these machines was out of the question.

I had seen in the yard of Captain Bishop's store at Port Lincoln, a little, common machine known as a timber-gin, which is extensively used in timber yards, shipbuilding yards, &c., and for stowing cargo in ships. It looks like a block of wood, perhaps about two feet six long, and about nine or ten inches broad. It has in it an arrangement of cogwheels by means of which a strong piece of iron called the sword is pushed out with great power from one end. It occurred to me that by fixing this up immediately over the wool bale, the sword might be pushed downward, and we might thereby obtain the necessary pressure. I therefore proceeded to work out the idea ; and I made a cardboard model of the structure I wished to be erected. It was simply a very massive gallows, strong enough and heavy enough to resist the upward pressure when the machine was putting forth its strength downward. I substituted staves, which could be worked by two men, for the ordinary windlass handle. A stage also was to be erected at the proper height on which the men were to stand to work the staves, the structure was set up under Mr. Wollaston's superintendence, according to the cardboard model. It answered admirably, and continued to be used for several seasons. In fact by means of it, we could put into a bale as many fleeces as the bale would contain without the danger of bursting. I forget what the limit is, but I think it is about 380 lbs. If somewhere about that weight is exceeded, the probability is that in consequence of the rough handling which the bale will meet with, it will burst before it reaches its destination.

I should have been glad if I could have given the names of the men who composed the party of shearers, but I cannot do so. In the year 1872, when I again visited Poonindie, I fell in, in the steamer, with a large flock owner, I believe the largest in the Port Lincoln district. He habitually employed the Poonindie shearers, and bore testimony to their usefulness and good conduct. He referred particularly to one of them, Tom Adams, and he said that there was not a man in the district that he liked better to see in his wool shed than Tom Adams. He is a half-caste and has a history, and I must here digress a little to tell it. I had heard of his father some time before I went to Poonindie. He was a shepherd in the employ of one of my great friends, at whose house I have very often stayed the night when on my journeys to and fro between Adelaide and the Clare district, where I was at one time stationed. This shepherd, Adams, had taken to wife a native woman, who had been brought up at some settler's station and was partially educated. Adams could not read, and the black wife taught the white husband to read. Two or three times I quoted this case when pleading the cause of the natives at public meetings in South Australia. It was in the year 1848 that I was frequently up and down that road, staying at night at the station referred to—Mr. Slater's.

In the month of May, in the year 1855, the man Adams made his appearance at Poonindie, bringing two little half-caste boys. He had come from Mr. Slater's station to Port Adelaide, and had then taken ship and come on by sea to Port Lincoln, for the purpose of asking me to take charge of his little boys. They were both sufficiently young to be baptized according to the form for Infant Baptism. They have grown up to be exemplary men and leading men in the Institution. And I hear that Tom, the eldest and the famous shearer, is now a grandfather. Of course I saw him on the occasion referred to, my visit of 1872, and a fine specimen of a man he is. He and his brother have thus been inmates of the Institution for very nearly thirty-four years.

The great farming event of each year, after the shearing, was the harvest, and I am sorry to say that, as I neglected my diary the latter part of 1853 and for several months afterwards, I am not able to give any account of the harvest of that year. My impression is that it was a fairly good one, and that it was got in, threshed, and cleaned, &c., by the natives, under Mr. Wollaston's superintendence.

I have made mention above of the achievement of the Poonindie men as shearers in after years, and I think I shall be excused if I make the following extract from the *Government Gazette*, of February 12, 1880, to show that they became accomplished ploughmen, as well as shearers, as time went on. Mr. Joseph Shaw, at that time super-intending the institution, reported to the Government as

follows :—" We have two or three very good ploughers,
" and, at a ploughing match in the district, some months
" ago, the natives succeeded in obtaining all the best
" prizes, much to the surprise of every one, particularly of
" the competitors, who were farmers of long standing in
" the district."

I find that, in consequence of my neglect of my diary, I
made a short summary of events connected with our
spiritual concerns in 1853 and the beginning of 1854. The
following is an extract of the summary :—" Most important
" have been the events which marked this period. What
" mercies have been showered down upon me ! How has
" God's goodness called upon me to devote myself more
" than ever to His service, with devoted zeal and singleness
" of purpose, and tenderness of spirit, in my endeavours to
" win souls to Christ. A mixture of sorrows and of joys in
" large measures has characterised the year : especially
" from our having been afflicted with so much sickness
" amongst the natives, and so many deaths. Most of them,
" however, watched the approach of the time for their re-
" spective departures out of this world, full of faith and hope.
" And, God be praised, they gave us every reason to
" believe that they were firmly established in the faith of
" Christ. In fact the state in which their minds were was
" such as nothing but the work of the Holy Spirit could
" have produced. Immediately connected with this sub-
" ject, and giving occasion for expressions of unbounded
" gratitude to the Giver of all good, is the progress which
" the work of God has been making during this period.
" The crowning point is that the natives now advise and
" exhort one another, and help one another."

Our dear friend Narrung died December 5. His was
the last death in 1853. For the reason already alleged, I
am not able to give any particulars of his last hours. I am
sure, however, that he died as I have represented him
above, a devout and earnest Christian. This much I distinctly remember, that when he had ceased to be able to
go to work, he used to sit in the open air with a cheerful
and happy look upon his face, reading his Testament ; *i.e.*,
the three or four chapters of St. John which he had learned
to read by going over them again and again. The seventeenth chapter was the one he especially loved. His usual
expression was that he was just waiting until it should
please God to call him.

I have now brought my narrative down to the end of 1853. I have entered much into details. My hope has been that I might so set the whole matter before the minds of my readers, that anyone who might think it worth while to make the effort, might almost fancy himself to be living and moving amongst us. He may surely pretty clearly understand how we were all occupied, and what was our general routine of employment from day to day. By the time we arrived at the end of the year 1853, that routine was firmly established by custom, and it appears to me that it is quite unnecessary for me to repeat the same things over and over again. I propose, therefore, to state only briefly the occurrences of the remaining time of my stay at Poonindie, concluding with a full account of the state of affairs at the time of my departure.

I have, in the course of my narrative, said much about the good conduct of our inmates and their progress in Christian knowledge and in the practice of Christian duties. But I have said nothing about the falls into sin of some amongst them. My silence on this last-named subject has by no means been occasioned by any desire to conceal the fact that there were falls into sin. But I have felt that to enter into details about these matters would be anything but edifying to the reader, and could not answer any good purpose. It must suffice therefore for me to say that we had cases of grievous falls. And what is, if possible, still more sad is, that we had grievous falls amongst my white assistants. In fact if by any possibility I could measure my trouble and distress of mind from the one source and from the other, it might be found that I had suffered almost more from the misconduct of some of the white people than from that of the natives. There was this difference. When the natives fell, they fell from a position which was new to them. They had had such a short time to accustom themselves to live up to the high standard of morals required by Christianity. They had had but a short time to learn and experience the utter help-lessness of man without the grace of God, and his liability to fall if he should neglect, even for the shortest time, diligently to seek that grace. The native fell. But his conscience was not outraged by sins done deliberately and of set purpose, in opposition to full light and knowledge.

The conscience therefore was not silenced: the offender was troubled in mind by its reproaches and the consequent remorse. The offender then became a penitent and rose again from his fall. In the case of the white offenders they put their hands to our work as persons having a zeal for religion. They sinned against the light and knowledge of many years. The conscience had been deliberately resisted; it had been reduced to silence: and there followed no sign of repentance.

1854.—The year 1854 was a year of marked character throughout the Colony of South Australia on account of the failure of the wheat crop. The long drought prevailing, I believe, over the whole Colony, produced the most disastrous results. At Poonindie, where there were so many mouths to be fed, this calamity affected us most seriously. It was not only from the failure of our own crop that we suffered; but the *general failure* ran up the price of flour to almost double what it had been when the Institution was first established. In 1850 and 1851 the price of flour ranged at about £11 or £12 per ton. After the failure of the wheat crop of 1854 the price went up to £20 per ton.

And this was not all. The owner of the little schooner which carried on the shipping trade between Port Adelaide and Port Lincoln raised enormously his charges for freight. These high prices lasted through nearly all the year 1855, and I was thereby greatly thrown back in my financial position. When I first started I had, of course, everything to do, and very insufficient funds to do it with, and I then got considerably into arrears. But, after I entered upon my contract, and had the £1,000 per annum, I was gradually picking up; and had nearly righted myself when the calamity of 1854 threw me back again. I here gratefully mention the name of Mr. Alexander Lang Elder—for he it was who sustained me in my difficulties, and enabled me to carry on my undertaking. I did all my business with him; and he, knowing how I was circumstanced, continued to send me flour and other provisions according to my need, when I had got far behind in my payments.

He, and Mrs. Elder and their little boy, taking a pleasure trip in one of his well-earned holidays, paid a visit to Port Lincoln; and I had the pleasure of driving them out to Poonindie to see our little settlement.

So far from being discouraged by the failure of the crop for 1854, we got more land than ever under cultivation in 1855, and it then pleased God to bless us with an abundant crop. We were able to send 600 bushels of wheat to Captain Hart's mill at Port Adelaide to be ground for the Institution, and 100 bushels were kept at home for seed or any other purpose for which it might be required.

I must now return to that subject which occupies so large a space in this narrative. In one of my official Reports to the Government, I wrote as follows : " I am most anxious " to leave no means untried to preserve our inmates in " health, and, if possible, to stay the tide of mortality which " seems to have set in upon us. With a view to the more " effectual use of such means as may be within our reach, " I am anxious to procure, for at any rate some months, the " services of a medical man to be resident at the Institu- " tion, who would then have it in his power to watch very " narrowly the health of the inmates ; and he might be able to " discover whether, amongst the peculiarities of their habits " and of their manner of life in this place, there is anything " which can be specially fixed upon as being detrimental to " health. To any person who may read this, and who will " endeavour to procure for me the benefit of such medical " aid, I shall feel really and sincerely indebted." I then mentioned the name of Mr. Moorhouse, and the names of two other leading medical men to whom communications might be addressed. I again returned to this subject in a later Report, and said : " I have still the same anxieties as " I before expressed to have the benefit of the temporary " residence of some medical man at the Institution ; but " I have received no communication from any quarter upon " the subject."

But that which I spoke of as a tide of mortality setting in upon us did not recede. We had many deaths in 1854 and 1855 ; but we had still the same consolations to support us as those already described. In the majority of cases those who left us departed full of Christian faith, hoping for a blessed resurrection. Having no diary of the period to refer to, I am not able to specify particulars, except in a few cases ; for, as may be supposed, there was much simi- larity in the cases. I have a distinct recollection, however, of one of my visits to the bedside of a dear lad named

Moonchie. He was a cheerful, good tempered fellow, much liked by his companions; but he was volatile, and had often needed reproofs. On the occasion I refer to, I had read to him the parable of the Prodigal Son, and was trying to bring home to him its application. I remarked upon the action of the father, as represented in the parable, and his fatherly love and readiness to forgive; and then I asked, "What does that mean?" He answered quite readily, "That means God." Then I remarked upon the action of the returning son, and was proceeding to ask the same question with reference to him. I have very often made use of the parable in the same way, when teaching young or simple-minded persons; and the answer about the son has been, so far I remember, invariably a general one, such as "That means the sinner praying for forgiveness of his " sins," and in such cases something more has to be said to make the application personal. But, in poor Moonchie's case, there was no need to get to the point in a round-about way. He scarcely gave me time to ask the question about the son, but replied quickly, and with much animation, " That's me." Moonchie was one of the fifteen whom I brought with me from Adelaide in January, 1852. He was baptized in August, 1853, and died in December, 1854.

I mention another case, that of Taaba, because she belonged to the Port Lincoln district, and was the first of that district who, as we hope, died in the faith. It will be remembered that, at Mr. Schürmann's urgent request, I received, before the school was transferred to Poonindie, three of his girls, who, as he said, had out-grown the school. Taaba was one of them; and for that reason I made special mention of her case in my Report to the Government of January, 1856. She was admitted to Poonindie, November, 1852; was baptized at the same time as Moonchie, August, 1853; and died December, 1855. This is what I said of her:—" She had uniformly "conducted herself with strict propriety. She was very " intelligent, and could read well, but she did not manifest " that degree of earnestness in the pursuit of the Kingdom " of Heaven, or that deep concern about the salvation of " her soul which I should have been thankful to have " witnessed. Her own relations, mother, &c., still living " for the most part in the Bush, and conforming to Bush

G

" habits of life, were constantly with her during her last
" illness; and their presence and companionship operated,
" I have no doubt, in a manner very unfavourable to her
" spiritual condition."

Dear, good Neechi, who died in August, 1855, had been truly a pillar of the Institution from the day of its foundation. He was one of those who had been sent by Mr. Moorhouse to be employed upon a station before I had anything to do with the matter. He and his wife Kilpa joined our party when we went to Boston Island. He was a man of different temperament from his great friend Narrung, less animated, and quiet in manner. But he sympathized, heart and soul, with his friend in every thing that was good. His services, in work of all kinds, were valuable, because he could always be thoroughly depended upon. And he was at home in occupations of every kind. I have no record of his last days, but I feel perfectly sure that he died, as he had lived, an earnest, consistent and devout Christian.

It appears that I did not, as a rule, preserve copies of my Reports to the Government, although I have been able to give extracts from some of them. The following extracts is from the Report of December 31, 1855 :—

" I have now to record the death of another whose loss we deeply feel.

" For a length of time, the exemplary conduct and unblemished character of *Joseph Mudlong* exercised a most important influence amongst the members of our little community. When I first made his acquaintance, at the beginning of 1851,he was a messenger at Government House known by the name of Jemmy. In June of that same year he joined the Institution. In February, 1853, on the occasion of the Bishop's visit to Poonindie, he, together with Neechi, Narrung and others, eleven in all, received the Sacrament of Baptism at his Lordship's hands. From first to last his conduct was most correct and blameless; but not only by this decorum and correct-ness of life was the reality of his Christian principles evidenced. It was manifest that his *heart* was with God. He was a lover of good things and one who yearned after the souls of others. He was ever forward to instruct the young and to guide and teach those who possessed less knowledge than himself. The man who, taking a less favoured brother for his pupil, unobserved by any eye but that of God, unbidden by any voice but that of Christian charity speaking within him, will affectionately strive for that brother's soul and patiently instruct him in the blessed way of salvation—that man must needs be a blessing to any community, and his departure from that community must needs be felt to be a heavy privation. Such was Joseph Mudlong at Poonindie. The day is yet future when the fruits of his spiritual labours will be fully known. His last days upon earth were strictly in keeping with those which had gone before. As the time approached for his departure to that Heavenly Kingdom, which he so earnestly desired, his disposition, habitually cheerful, became more so than usual; and, notwithstanding his sufferings and extreme debility, there was a tone of happiness, I may indeed say of joyousness, pervading his whole mind, which was most edifying to all about him. We shall greatly feel his loss. In the school, as well as elsewhere, he rendered important aid; and frequently on Sundays, as well as upon other days, he conducted Divine Service in my absence.

" I bear in mind in this case, as I have done upon similar occasions before, that I am writing an *Official Report*, and, therefore, I abstain from saying more than I feel to be necessary to show that the Institution is satisfactorily accomplishing the great object for which it was formed, viz., that of leading on the inmates step by step to a knowledge of their Crucified Redeemer, and preparing them to enter into everlasting life. We now reckon something like seventeen or eighteen souls, once members of our little community, whom we firmly believe to have entered into their heavenly rest.

" Of the peculiar features and characteristics of their piety I could say much if I considered this a proper place for such enlargement. One feature, however, I must remark upon, viz., the clear and unclouded happiness of their minds as death approaches. For nearly twenty years the duties of my sacred calling have brought me much into the presence of the sick and dying. In my ministrations amongst persons in this condition I feel that my Divine Master has enabled me to reap my richest fruits. Yet the calm, uninterrupted happiness at the approach of death, such as that which I have just described, I have met with in *comparatively* but few instances amongst those of my own race. A lurking worldliness of mind, a hankering after and a care for ' many things '—how often do these enemies of the Christian's peace disturb his mind and cast a cloud over his happiness as his great change draws near. At the death-bed of Joseph Mudlong, and others of his race who have gone before him, I have felt, indeed, constrained to exclaim, ' Let me die the death of the righteous, and let my last end be like his.' "

I have now brought to a conclusion my part of the story of Poonindie. For the second part we are to be indebted to the pen of Mr. Edwin Blackmore, Clerk of the Legislative Council of South Australia. Mr. Blackmore possesses every qualification requisite for the performance of this task. He is not only intimately acquainted with Poonindie and all connected with the place, he is also officially connected with the Institution, having been for the past eight years the acting Trustee thereof, and he is thoroughly accustomed to literary work. The second part will be of great interest and importance, because it will show that the Institution has a vitality of its own. Like all human institutions, it has had its ups and downs. Many hands and many minds have been connected with its management, but it has still kept steadily on its way for a period of nearly forty years, doing its work for God's glory and for the salvation of souls.

Many readers of my narrative may like to know what strangers have thought and said about Poonindie. I therefore add four Appendices. Appendix A is a letter written by a gentleman named Lowe, who stayed with us a short time a few weeks before my departure. Mr. Lowe's expressions and his whole earnest demeanour made it manifest that his visit made a very deep impression upon him.

About Mr. Goodwin, the writer of the letter, Appendix B, I never had any information except that which I derived from newspapers. My impression is that he travelled from Melbourne for the express purpose of visiting Poonindie, and that he was requested to do this, either on behalf of some religious society or as a representative of the press. All that I could learn about the writer of the paper in Appendix C was that he was a stranger who visited the Port Lincoln district. *The Melbourne Missionary*, in which the paper appeared, is a little religious periodical, edited by the Rev. Hussey de Burgh Macartney, of Melbourne. The paper, Appendix D, with the heading, sufficiently explains itself.

APPENDIX A.

A VISIT TO POONINDIE.

The following is an extract from a letter written to Archdeacon Hale by a gentleman, long resident in the Colony of New South Wales, who, early in the year 1856, visited the Natives' Training Institution at Poonindie, Port Lincoln :—

" I could not, after the termination of a long journey across this vast country from E. to W., along a line of rivers on whose banks abundant examples of the aboriginal population are to be seen and studied in their habits and condition, witness what I saw at Poonindie, and in connection with your Training Institution, without a deep impression of the wonderful work it has accomplished. I say wonderful, because at every stage of my journey I made, as opportunity occurred, and such was almost daily, minute inquiries as to the gradually wasting away of tribes of men once occupiers of the soil, and the progress of the remnant that was left—in European habits, general civilization, moral and religious improvement, as also as to their food, their dress, their superstitions—the results of contact with the white man—their intelligence, their capabilities; and the result was that each day added to the hopelessness I felt of any such change as would rescue them from the degraded condition that everywhere, in one shape or another, was presented. I became conscious of the amount of depravity that was conquered only when I contrasted the wretchedness to which I have averted with the comforts you have bestowed on the aboriginal natives under your personal care, as evidenced by the condition of those around you.

" I think you had sixty inmates when I visited your institution; and when I saw the adult members of your flock pursuing the avocations of the farm, conscious of the self-respect which man owes to himself as a rational being, well clothed (by means of their own earnings), quiet, orderly, deferential yet not servile, supplying the place of my own countrymen (without their vices) in shearing the plough, with the sickle, as shepherds, standing out in strong relief from the wild tribes around them, I then felt that the objection was for ever silenced that the aboriginal is not to be reclaimed. He stood before me as an example of a good and useful member of society; but that was not all. I saw not only his social improvement, but the cultivation of religion bearing its fruits—in some thirty, in some an hundredfold. My feelings are not readily to be described when, as your guest, I heard the matins bell summoning the village to early worship; and, obeying its call, I found your chapel benches filled by civilized and baptized natives, who were repeating in my own tongue the responses of my own Church, and listening reverentially to the portion of the Scripture she dispenses to them daily, and observing a demeanour which would put many of those white men to shame, who, when they enter a church, are there ashamed to kneel. Not only by outward posture, but with heartfelt earnestness, did these men reverence the sanctuary. I heard the tone of their repetition of the Confession. I heard the voice of their psalmody and thanksgivings in the accents of our own Church music, accompanied by their flutes, and I acknowledged that they were there my teachers. Here, then, was the further proof that these difficult and blind tribes can be brought to the light of faith, and can evidence it by their lives. Let no man henceforth say they have neither part nor lot with us in the salvation vouchsafed to all! And, as these things were thus passing before me, one there was in your hospital, whose hours were numbered, even then praying for the conversion of his tribe."

APPENDIX B.

CHURCH OF ENGLAND MISSION TO THE ABORIGINES.

The following narrative of Mr. Goodwin's was read at the annual meeting of the members and friends of this Mission on the 19th Jan., 1860 :—

" I arrived at Port Lincoln (by the steamer *Marion*) on Sunday afternoon, November 27. The Bishop of Adelaide having kindly furnished me with an introduction to a Mr. Bishop, I at once directed my steps towards his residence, and there met with the Rev. O. Hammond, the superintendent of the Native Training Institution at Poonindie, who welcomed me in a very cordial manner. After a short delay, we started on horseback for Poonindie, which lies ten miles to the north of the town of Port Lincoln. The road lay along the shores of the noble harbour of Boston Bay, and for the first few miles over hills thickly timbered with sheoak to the water's edge, the country becoming more level and open as we neared Poonindie, which is situated a short distance from the banks of a small river named the Tod, upon a plain lightly timbered with sheoak, which is the prevailing timber of the country.

"The village of Poonindie consists of the superintendent's residence, and sundry out-buildings, a large stone building, used as a dining-hall by the natives, eight brick cottages (mostly two-roomed), and a schoolroom, which is 36 feet long by 16 feet wide inside, with a bay-window of four lights 4 feet deep; the side-walls are 17 feet high, the gable-ends 28 feet high: on one of them is a bellturret; it is built of stone with brick quoins, and forms a prominent and pleasing object in the view of the village, as seen from a distance.

"We arrived at Poonindie at 6 o'oclock p.m.; at 7 the bell was rung for evening service, when all the adult native population and other residents assembled in the schoolroom, forming a congregation of about 35 to 40 persons.

"The Rev. O. Hammond read service, the whole congregation joining in the responses, in a devout and intelligent manner, confessing that they had 'done those things which they ought not to have done, and left undone those things which they ought to have done:' reading in an audible yet subdued voice the alternate verses of the Psalms, the 'Magnificat' and 'Deus Misereatur;' professing their belief in God the Father, the Son, and the Holy Ghost; and uniting in singing the praises of our Lord and Saviour—the singing being led by two men (aborigines) playing on flutes from written music before them, in a manner highly creditable to themselves, and most pleasing to hear. The hymn sung was 'Lo! He comes in clouds descending.' Mr. Hammond, in a simple and impressive manner, addressed them on the subject of Our Lord's second coming, and the service concluded by singing the hymn, 'Lord, dismiss us with Thy blessing.'

"I never saw a more quiet, orderly and attentive congregation. I had heard and read some little of what was done at Poonindie, but I was scarcely prepared for what I witnessed there. Here were these who by many persons are deemed but one remove above 'the beasts that perish,' reckoned almost beneath the notice of the Almighty, incapable of civilization, unsusceptible of religious impressions, and hopelessly sunk in ignorance, barbarism, and sensuality—here were these, a remnant, it is true, but yet a people 'clothed and in their right mind,' worshipping Him whom their fathers knew not, but who, by His all powerful grace, they have been brought to know and love.

"What I saw filled me with much joy—my heart overflowed—tears filled my eyes—I 'thanked God and took courage.'

"On Monday morning, at seven o'clock, the bell was rung for prayers, at which most of the people attended, when a chapter from the Old Testament and a selection of prayers from the Liturgy were read. After breakfast the men and boys went about the business of the farm. Most of them were employed in cutting hay, which was carted home during the week, the whole being done by them without any superintendence. At eleven o'clock the women and children assembled in the schoolroom for instruction. I heard them read from their lesson books, and also from the New Testament, and many of them gave suitable replies to questions that were addressed to them, and nearly all of them are acquainted with the Church Catechism.

"In the afternoon they again met to be taught sewing, in addition to reading and writing. The evening school, conducted by Mr. Hammond, was well attended by men and boys; many of them can read and write very well, and are able to give intelligent replies to questions proposed to them on what they have read. The cleanly state of their copy-books, and the uniform progress of their improvement in writing, would do credit to any school. All, of course, are not equally talented, some making more rapid progress and taking greater delight in their work than others.

"At about half-past eight the bell was rung, when the adult population assembled in the schoolroom for evening prayer. A hymn was sung, a chapter from the New Testament and a selection of prayers from the Liturgy read; and thus was the day brought to a conclusion in a profitable, peaceful, and Christian-like manner. The same course of procedure is gone through daily, except during shearing time, when the school is necessarily interrupted.

" On Tuesday I inspected the premises, and went over a part of the run. The natives' cottages are built of brick, and thatched. Most of them contain two separate rooms, about 9 by feet 7, with fireplace in each, and form a residence for two families. All the cottages were in a cleanly and tidy condition, and in nearly all I saw a small shelf, on which were a few well-used books, and most prominent of all was the New Testament, which I was told they prefer to any other, generally taking that in preference to any other book when they go to any of the out-stations to shepherd. The run comprises 35 square miles, and the stock consists of a little more than 6,000 (six thousand) sheep, about 300 (three hundred) cattle, and from 40 to 50 horses.

" The expenses of building have hitherto required an annual grant from Government, which last year was reduced from £1,000 to £500. With the above-mentioned stock, it is thought and hoped by many that the time is near when the Institution will be altogether self-supporting, and independent of the Government grant. A portion of the land is cultivated, but only 15 acres are under wheat this year, and owing to the very dry season, it will be but a very poor crop. On Wednesday there was a flock of sheep to be drafted. I went to the sheepyards, and when the drafting was done the sheep were counted out of the yard by one of the blacks. Placing myself in a convenient position, I also counted the sheep, but without his being aware that I was doing so. When the whole were counted I found that he had counted them quite correctly; the flock numbered over 1,500 (fifteen hundred).

" Who will say after this that the aborigines are incapable of mental improvement ?

" With regard to their spiritual improvement there is cause for much thankfulness. Many have given good evidence, both in their life and by their death, that the saving truths of our most holy religion have found a place in their hearts—their sorrow for sin, their faith in Christ's atonement, their forgiveness of injuries, their love to their fellow-men, and earnest desire that they should be taught the truth as it is in Jesus, have proved in those that have departed to their rest, and yet prove in those that remain, the sincerity of their faith in Christ.

I would not, however, be understood to say that they have attained to all that we desire to see them—that they are 'model Christians.' I think people in general expect too much from all missionary efforts, and because they do not see the heathen converts, and especially the aborigines of this country, attain to the perfect model of Christian life and practice which they think they should, they are, if friendly to missions, discouraged ; or, on the other hand, if unfriendly, they at once say it is useless to attempt either conversion or improvement.

" Let us, however, 'judge righteous judgment ; ' let us contrast the present state of the inmates of the Institution at Poonindie with that of the natives in the Bush, with that in which their forefathers lived—yea, contrast their state, their lives, and conduct with those of many of our own people who have had advantages far exceeding any that the poor aborigines have had—and I say the contrast will be much in favour of the inhabitants of Poonindie. If 'all who profess and call themselves Christians' were practical Christians, as well as professing Christians we should hear less about the impossibility of converting the aborigines ; less about the inutility of any efforts for their civilization, and more about the good that has been effected by the few and feeble efforts that have been made for their improvement and well being, and those efforts, instead of being discouraged and deprecated, would be lauded and redoubled.

" As an instance that the instruction given at Poonindie is not in vain, I heard of a woman who a few years ago was dismissed from the Institution for ill conduct. A few months since she was employed at a station some miles distant, and while there was taken ill and died. Her last words were, ' Tell the boys I have not forgotten what I learned at Poonindie—tell the boys I have not forgotten what I learned at Poonindie.' The seed sown had taken root, rugged though the soil was ; and may we not hope that though the day of her life was dark and cloudy, that at 'eventide there was light ? '

" I remained at Poonindie a week, and during that time had ample opportunities of observing the character and conduct of its forty-five inhabitants—a more peaceable, orderly, and contented community there cannot be ; and taking into consideration their want of stamina, and their inability to endure long-continued labour (and also the natural indolence of the race, which cannot be eradicated in one generation or two), they are on the whole industrious.

"I shall ever look back with pleasure to my week's sojourn amongst them, and with grateful recollection of the kind and openhearted hospitality shown me by Mr. Hammond and his family.

"I left Poonindie at five o'clock on the morning of Sunday, December 4, and arrived at Port Lincoln in time for the steamer to Adelaide."—*Argus.*

APPENDIX C.

The following account of the Poonindie Native Settlement, South Australia, is from *The Melbourne Missionary* :—

"What a curious village! No public-house and no gaol or police-barracks! Here in this arcadia the little community, men, women, and children, morning and evening, meet in church for prayer and praise. None of its members ever go to law ; no drunkenness or crime is here found, and should any little dispute arise it is settled among themselves in a Christian manner, in accordance with St. Paul's instructions to the Corinthians. There is an educational establishment, where some of the pupils can show creditable specimens of penmanship, &c. Singing classes for practising sacred music are held in the church. Everybody looked fat, happy and clean. One of the laws is that every one must have a hot bath every Saturday evening, and a cold one as often as he or she likes. The curfew-bell tolls a little later than under the Norman rule, and when it rings lights are put out and all retire to rest. Every morning the men proceed to their rural avocations—some reaping, some shepherding, some building. Meantime the wives are washing and cooking, and the children learning and playing, and on the Sabbath they listen in their beloved church to their pastor, and chant their *glorias* and anthems and sing hymns in a beautiful manner. Now, who are those people living in such an orderly and exemplary manner? The despised aborigines of South Australia.

Those farmers who with their families, take a pleasure in every morning meeting in church to ask God's blessing on the day, and in the evening return thanks in the same

manner, whose lives and conduct may compare favourably
with the squirearchy of the last century, are the race that
has furnished examples of degraded humanity to every
author treating of the variety of the various divisions of the
human race. It is impossible to visit Poonindie Institution
without being deeply interested. The problem whether
aborigines can be civilized or not is here solved ; and mind,
no partial civilization, no mixing up of Christian and pagan
usages here ; no carrying about of dead bodies, as is allowed
elsewhere ; no fear of offending by decidedly preventing any
pagan and filthy usages ; but a firm, kind control, under
which order and harmony prevail. These people are not
the lazy recipients of State aid or private benevolence.
Everyone of ability has to work, and so fond are they of the
mode of life that the greatest punishment that can be in-
flicted upon them is to threaten to send them away. Of
course this order and almost perfection did not come at
once. The present superintendent, Mr. W. R. Holden, is
much beloved by the natives.

Appendix D.

An extract from an account of a visit to Poonindie in
year 1872, written by the Bishop (Dr. Short) of Adelaide.

" For five happy years, under the Archdeacon's personal direction, this growth, material and spiritual, continued. In spite of about twenty deaths—not less than
seventeen of which were attended with circumstances
justifying a very happy hope of the state of the departed—
the numbers in the Institution reached sixty-two. They
are now eighty-three, and the difficulties which beset it at
an earlier period seemed in great measure to have been
removed. The natives were moral in their conduct, and
able to resist temptation when sent with drayloads into
Port Lincoln. It is remembered how " Conwillan " on one
occasion having loaded his own dray with goods from a
coasting vessel according to orders, was found by the
Archdeacon rendering the like service to a settler, whose
teamster was lying intoxicated on the beach; and in no
one single instance did it happen that a Poonindie native,
sent upon errands into the township, was ever found ' the
worse for liquor,' however frequently sent there upon
business. At that time drunkenness was the constant and
prevailing sin of the white labourers.

" The Sunday services meanwhile, and daily worship carried on at the Poonindie Chapel, were marked with so much reverence and devotional fervour, that the 'strangers' from Adelaide or elsewhere became most favourably impressed with the sincerity of that worship, and the piety of spirit from which it emanated. The singing was led by three of the elder young men playing on flutes, while the low gentle voices of the others made their ' psalms and hymns and spiritual songs ' a delight to themselves and all who heard them.

Time at length brought its vicissitudes. In June, 1856, Archdeacon Hale was called, in the Providence of God, to fill the See of Perth, in Western Australia, which was at that time made a separate diocese from Adelaide. The removal of the founder—the spiritual and temporal head of the Institution, the friend and guide, the teacher and counsellor, the example and ruler of the natives, could not but be a sorrowful event. It might have been disastrous. The loss of a loving Christian father must needs be distressing to his children. Poonindie was not exempted from the sadness and ill effects of such a deprivation.

" The difficulty, nay, impossibility of finding one to succeed the Bishop of Perth, as deeply interested as himself in the Mission, as well as qualified to conduct its complicated details, was quickly discovered. Even if the like Christian temper and benevolence might be hoped for, it was not easy to find a missionary his equal in knowledge of men and things ; of business habits, and having a general acquaintance with the details of sheep and cattle management as well as farming. The expenses of the establishment were to be defrayed in part out of the proceeds of the sheep and farm. Then followed a season of severe sickness, under which, during two years, month after month, the elder natives were struck down. Between July, 1856, and March, 1858, in spite of all Mr. Hammond's skill, watchfulness, and care, twenty-one deaths ensued. The cloud of sorrow lay dark and heavy upon the Institution. The spirit of the inmates sank ; a rumour of the mortality had reached their friends in the Bush, and none were inclined to enter what seemed to them the ' valley of the shadow of death.'

" Other discouragements succeeded. The House of Assembly refused to vote supplies for its support, although a new Trustee had been chosen, and an Overseer, directly responsible to the Government, had, at the instance of the Chief Secretary, been appointed. Rumours became rife of revocation of the native reserve; of the putting up for sale the land marked out in sections: of mismanagement; and that, associated with utter unbelief in the public mind generally of any possible benefit from the Institution to the natives; complaints from the natives themselves of harsh and unfair treatment from the Overseer. To obviate such complaints and secure some fruit of their labour beyond food, raiment, and clothing, the Trustees arranged that a weekly money payment should be placed to their account, which they might spend as they themselves chose. The system thus inaugurated was found to work well, as it had, at an earlier period, under the Archdeacon. It has since been continued and extended.

"It was pleasing to observe how well, generally speaking, the money was spent: in procuring good clothes for themselves and wives, or domestic comforts, or paying passage money by steamer to Adelaide, and spending there, with all propriety of conduct, a short holiday. Health and quietness seemed once more to come back to the Institution, which prospered in a worldly sense under the skilful management of the Overseer; but the higher tone and happier spirit of the primitive period were lacking. The Superintendent acting in the name of the Church, and the Overseer exercising authority over the natives on behalf of the Government, the usual consequences of divided responsibility followed; and while the Station prospered, the Mission was overshadowed. During this period, however, the school was kept up by Mr. Hammond and his daughter, and then taken charge of by two theological students in succession during two-years-and-a-half—the Revs. W. Clayfield and F. S. Poole—who did good service, maintaining discipline and good conduct among the younger inmates.

" A change at length took place on the appointment as Trustee of Mr. G. W. Hawkes—a name well-known in Sydney and Adelaide for zealous co-operation in every work of benevolence. The Governor having ratified his nomination by the Lord Bishop of Adelaide, the Institution was carried on after his appointment in the joint names of the present Trustees—the Lord Bishop of Adelaide, Samuel Davenport, and G. W. Hawkes, Esqs.

" Once more it became possible, by a change in the management, to restore the *missionary* character of the Institution, and realize the grand idea of the founder, viz. : —a Christian village of South Australian natives, reclaimed from barbarism, trained to the duties of social Christian life, and walking in the fear of God, through knowledge and faith in the love of Christ their Saviour ; and the power of His Spirit.

" It is unnecessary to trace the steps by which, in June, 1868, the existing arrangements were brought into full working order under the present staff of officers :—

" The Rev. O. Hammond, Chaplain (charged also with inspection of the sanitary condition of the natives).

" Mr. Robert William Holden, Superintendent and Instructor. (Mrs. Holden subsequently took charge of the women and girls.)

" Mr. Watts Newland, Managing Overseer of the Station.

" The object of employing only *native* labour in the operations of the farm and run being kept in view, as few white people were engaged as possible, viz., a carpenter, a ploughman, and a station cook, who baked for the natives.

" The ordinary routine of daily employment then adopted is as follows :—

" At six a.m. the station-bell rings. The natives having charge of teams go to the stables to feed and water their horses. The bullocks and horses required for the day are brought in by the stockmen. At seven the Chapel-bell is rung for morning prayer, when all the inmates of the Institution are expected to attend. There is seldom occasion to find fault with the attendance. During the months of September and October of the present year, 1872, 60 adults are recorded as present both morning and evening, *besides* children, out of a total of 86 natives. At half-past seven, breakfast ; the single men and boys breakfasting together in their kitchen ; the single women and girls also by themselves ; the married couples in their cottages. In winter, the time is one half-hour later.

" At eight a.m. the station *work-bell* is rung and the workmen go to their different employments varying with the season—such as ploughing, when six teams are generally at work, five under natives; harrowing, sowing, tending the mowing or reaping machine, fencing, grubbing—the two latter *exclusively* by natives—the former partially, being under the direction of the ploughman. The run being fenced, four natives are employed as boundary riders to keep the fences in order. In the lambing season natives only are employed—mustering, cutting, branding, drafting both sheep and cattle. At the shearing season they wash, shear, press, and cart the wool bales to the shipping place.

" At twelve the dinner-bell rings for the whole establishment; at one, work is resumed on the bell being rung; at six in the summer and five in winter the labours of the day cease; at half-past seven p.m. evening prayer is read by the Superintendent, with a lesson from Scripture, and two hymns are sung; at nine the single boys and girls are mustered at the Mission House, and then retire to their respective dormitories—the married couples soon after. Such is the general routine of the day for the working population.

" If it is asked in what way the natives are remunerated for their labour, the following system is in full and satisfactory operation :—For day work from 10s. per week to 12s. are paid, according to ability; at machine work or ploughing, £1 per week; shearing, 15s. per 100, the same as whites. The two best native shearers earned each £14 in a month during the present season.

" Besides the above wages the following is the ration allowance :—Sugar, 2 lbs. a week for each adult; tea, ¼ lb. ; flour, 10 lbs. ; rice, 1 lb. ; tobacco, four sticks to each man; soap, 1 lb. ; meat, 10 lbs. ; bacon, 1½ lbs. ; honey, treacle, oatmeal as required. If sick, sago, maizena, and other medical comforts are supplied gratis. Half the above scale is adopted for children.

" With regard to schooling, all the children who need to be instructed, not being allowed to go to work, are assembled in the schoolroom from 9 to 11 a.m., and 2 to 3 in the afternoon. A sewing class assembles at the same time, when Mrs. Holden instructs the women and girls.

" In the evening there is school for adults and boys from 6.30 to 7.30, at which hour the chapel bell rings for prayers. The whole number under instruction averages thirty. Their reading is intelligent; writing very fair; the arithmetic does not go beyond the four first rules. There are also maps, Scripture plates, and others for teaching natural history.

" One evening in the week a sewing class assembles at the Mission House, the work being paid for according to skill, and the proceeds devoted to some charitable or missionary object. Mrs. Holden then reads to the women as they work. The average number attending is fifteen. Out of the funds thus collected, £1 was sent in July, 1872, to the Mayor of Glenelg in aid of the fund *then* being collected for two widows of boatmen, who were about that time drowned. It should also be mentioned that £10 is annually subscribed by the native men and women to maintain one Melanesian scholar at the Isle of Mota in the school established under Rev. George Sarawia by the lamented Bishop Patteson. Towards the debt on St. John's, Auburn, a sum of £2 15s. was also contributed.

" Linen for the Communion table—the finest which could be procured in the Colony—has been recently purchased by them, and their gratitude towards their Founder has lately manifested itself in the purchase of a tea service for presentation to him on his late visit to Poonindie, at the cost of £10.

" Amusements.—The experience of twenty-five years has shown that the native temperament is soon depressed by continuous labour, to which they have never been habituated. Their spirits flag; they become ill and restless; they long for change of scene, and thus are tempted to stray back into the Bush. Cricketing, therefore, was introduced with great success, and the Poonindie eleven has been with one exception successful in the matches with their white rivals at Port Lincoln. With the same object the schoolroom is thrown open every evening, when bagatelle, drafts, and other games (cards only excepted) are allowed. Music is a favourite pursuit. More than nine have learned to play the concertina; the flute and violin are also heard among them. Occasionally a few couples amuse themselves with dancing, and that with grace and decorum. A hornpipe danced by two of the men was remarkable for the precision of time. At nine o'clock the room is closed.

" At the time of writing this account, nothing can be more satisfactory than the *health* of every single native in the Institution—men, women, boys, girls, children, and infants. Of the last there are at this time fifteen, and the

H

comparative barrenness which for years hung over this, as over other native mission institutions, has been removed. This effect may probably be immediately traced to the higher moral, spiritual, and mental development of the inmates, and an improved physical condition resulting from such training. It is most pleasing to witness the affectionate relations of the married couples, and their great fondness for their children. The bright, happy playfulness of the latter, and the propriety of their behaviour, is a source of extreme pleasure to those who watch their free and unconstrained good-humour. There is very seldom indeed *any* dispute or quarrelling among them.

" We shall close this brief narrative with some account of the visit of the Bishop of Perth (after an absence of sixteen years) to the Institution which he had founded, and of a Sunday spent at Poonindie. Under the able management of Mr. Hawkes, it had been entirely relieved from debt, and all necessary improvements effected. The run had been fenced in, paddocks made, 200 acres cleared and ploughed, cottages built, schoolroom and dormitories erected, and the chapel repaired and beautified. An air of neatness and comfort pervaded the whole place. The whitewashed cottages—some with garden plots—were all tidy and clean within and without. The joyous looks of the natives on welcoming their first friend (though few only remained of those who had been under his personal care) sufficiently showed their grateful sense of what he had done for them. There was a full attendance at evening prayer, and a visit to some of the cottages and older married natives after service soon satisfied him of the *advance* made in their domestic and social habits, and consequent comfort and happiness. On Thursday, November 21, the schoolroom having been tastefully decorated with flowers and evergreens by the natives and half-castes themselves, at 7 o'clock their presentation of a tea service to the Bishop of Perth took place. An address was read on their behalf by Mr. Holden, to which the Bishop replied in his usual simple and feeling manner. The Bishop of Adelaide then read a letter concerning the Melanesian Mission, written by Mr. Codrington, on board the mission schooner, the *Southern Cross*, on the anniversary of Bishop Patteson's death, September 20, 1871. It stated that the visits of the mission ship were still gladly received by the natives, and that *one more* island had been added to the list of those which gladly received the Word of God. This intelligence caused much pleasure, showing that the *Poonindie contribution* of £10 annually to the mission fund was well and usefully bestowed. The pastoral staff given to the Bishop of Adelaide by the clergy and laity on completing the twenty-fifth year of his Episcopate, was then shown to them, many of the natives having contributed a trifle towards its purchase. On Saturday, the wool-carting having been completed, and the hay mown and cocked, a half-holiday was employed in cricketing, at which the young men are adepts, rarely failing to catch or pick up and throw with accuracy the ball.

" On Sunday the 24th, the Bishop of Perth took the morning services at 7 a.m. and 11. The first lesson for the day proved to be Ecclesiastes xi., which opens with words singularly appropriate to the occasion—' Cast thy bread upon the waters : and thou shalt find it after many days.' On this topic the Bishop dwelt in his discourse, and there was scarcely a dry eye in the assembly. The natives and half-castes were deeply impressed with the signal fulfilment of this promise to their founder and benefactor, while he himself could not but thankfully recognise the hand of God in all that has been accomplished. Many of the white neighbours also were present, and when the Bishop administered Holy Communion, *twenty-one* of the *aboriginal* inmates presented themselves to receive from his hands the emblems of their Redeemer's sacrifice. It was a season of refreshment much to be remembered at Poonindie, and encouraging alike to themselves and their spiritual guides and overseers. In the evening the Bishop of Adelaide (who had held a Confirmation in the morning at St. Thomas's, Port Lincoln) officiated. There was again a full attendance at service, and the hearty manner in which all responded and sang the hymns would have surprised as well as gratified all who believe the Gospel to be the power of God unto salvation.

" It remains only to add that the station was all astir at six a.m. on Monday morning. After full attendance in the Chapel, and breakfast, the whole establishment, men, women, and children, proceeded—some on foot, some by dray—to the shores of Louth Bay, about four miles from Poonindie, to see the wool bales (100) shipped on board the steamer *Lubra*. In 1871 the Poonindie wool fetched 1s. 8½d. per lb. The shipping day is always a kind of *red letter* festival in the simple calendar of the Station, but this occasion was more than usually interesting, because the Poonindie eleven were to embark for Adelaide to play a cricket match with the scholars of the Collegiate School of St. Peter. To those who have any doubts as to the identity of the manhood in the white and black-skinned races, it may be satisfactory to learn that the same *hopes* and *fears*, the same *zeal for the honour* of the Institution, the same *pride* in the cricketing *uniform* and *colours*, the same self-complacent *vanity* in looking 'the thing,' the same, it may be, *affectionate pride* on the part of the dark-skinned 'loving wife' in the appearance at Adelaide of her 'well got-up' husband, animated on this occasion the *quondam denizens* of the wilderness; as the like feelings annually manifest themselves on the part of mothers and sisters of old—Etonians and Harrovians at the cricket matches at Lord's proving incontestably that the Anglican aristocracy of England and the 'noble savage' who ran wild in the Australian woods are linked together in *one brotherhood of blood*—moved by the same passions, desires, and affections; differing only because in His wisdom God has ordained that His revealed truth, made known first to a Syrian, ready to perish, from 'Ur of the Chaldees,' should travel *westward* from the hills and valleys of Canaan; until at the appointed time the stream of Divine knowledge should turn eastward, and cover the whole earth 'as the waters cover the sea.' It may suffice to lower the pride of the white-skinned race to know, that the half-caste children between the high Caucasian Englishman and the (supposed) *degraded* Australian type of humanity are a fine, powerful, healthy, good-looking race—both men and women; not darker than the natives of Southern Europe, and capable in all respects of taking their place even in the first generation beside the Briton or Teuton; driving the plough, or wielding the axe with *equal* precision, or shearing with *greater* care and skill—from 75 to 100 sheep a day—than their *white* competitors. It is well known in the Port Lincoln district that the Poonindie shearers do their work most satisfactorily, and that Tom Adams is considered the best shearer in the whole district. Let prejudice then give way before the inexorable logic of facts, and let the 'caviller,' if he can, point out a hamlet of equal numbers, composed of natives from different districts of Great Britain and Ireland, so dwelling together in peace and harmony, and equally free from moral offences, or so attentive to their religious duties, as are the natives and half-castes now living in the Institution at Poonindie; enjoying consequently much happiness, and walking in the fear of God. To Him be all the glory, through Jesus Christ our Lord.

" AUGUSTUS ADELAIDE."

THE END.

LONDON:
PRINTED BY PERRY, GARDNER AND CO.,
FARRINGDON ROAD, E.C.

PUBLICATIONS

OF THE

Society for Promoting Christian Knowledge.

———— ◆ ————

FOR MISSIONS (AT HOME AND ABROAD).

A Missionary Brotherhood in the Far West; or, the Story of Nashotah.

Fcap. 8vo., covers, 6d.

[A Memorial of the Foundation and Work of an Associate Mission and Theological Seminary of the American Church: for General Readers.]

A Suffolk Boy in East Africa.

18mo. With Illustrations. Cloth boards, 9d.

[An Account of the Work of a Young Missionary on the East Coast of Africa; an incentive to Mission Work: for Young Lads.]

A Trial of Faith ; or, Adventures in a Mission Station in Labrador.

18mo., paper cover, 2d.

[A Story of Hardships experienced at a Mission Station in Labrador: for Young People.]

Addresses to English Men and English Women in India.

By the Bishops of Calcutta, Madras, and Bombay. Fcap. 8vo., paper cover, 1d.

[For Parochial Distribution among the Better Classes.]

Adjai; or, the True Story of a Little African Slave Boy.

18mo., with an Illustration. Paper cover, 1d.

[Tells how a Slave Boy became a Bishop of the Church in Africa: for Young Readers.]

Aunt Hilda's Story.

18mo., paper cover, 3d.

[An Account of Mission Work in the Deccan: for Young People.]

Christian Missions before the Reformation.

By the Rev. F. F. WALROND, M.A. Post 8vo., with four illustrations, cloth boards, 2s. 6d. [For General Readers.]

Christian Missions of the Middle Ages; or, A Thousand Years.

By the late Rev. JOHN WYSE. 8vo., with four illustrations, cloth boards, 2s.

[Principally suited for Educated Persons.]

Distant Brethren of Low Degree; or, Missionary Gleanings in Southern Africa.

By the Rev. JOHN WIDDICOMBE, of the South Becuanaland Mission. 18mo., paper cover, 4d.

[Exhibits the Effect of Grace on Individuals of the Lowest Races: for General Readers, Young and Old.]

Early Missions to and within the British Islands.

By the Rev. C. HOLE, B.A. Post 8vo., cloth boards, 2s.

[The History of British Missions from the Introduction of Christianity till the time of Archbishop Theodore.]

Klatsassan, and other Reminiscences of Missionary Life in British Columbia.

By the Rev. R. C. LUNDIN BROWN, M.A. Post 8vo., with Map and three illustrations on toned paper. Cloth boards, 2s.

[A Book of Adventure : for General Readers.]

Mission Heroes.

Bishop Patteson, Missionary, Bishop, and Martyr.
Bishop Field, of Newfoundland.
Bishop Steere, of Zanzibar.
Bishop Selwyn.
Bishop Cotton, of India.
Bishop Gray.   Crown 8vo., 1d. each.

[A Series of Lives of the principal Workers in the Mission field.]

Mission Tales in Verse.

By the Rev. F. W. MANT, B.A., with several illustrations. Fcap. 8vo., paper cover, 4d.

[The Stories told are interesting in themselves, and calculated to excite among the Young interest in Mission Work.]

Mission Work among the Indian Tribes in the Forests of Guiana.

By the Rev. W. H. BRETT, B.D., with map and illustrations. Crown 8vo., cloth boards, 3s.

[An interesting and valuable Account of Mission Work among the Natives of Guiana, by one who has spent half a lifetime there: for the Parochial Library.]

Missionary Work among the Ojebway Indians.

By the Rev. E. F. WILSON, with numerous illustrations. Post 8vo., cloth boards, 2s. 6d.

[An interesting Account of Mission Work among the Ojebway Indians, giving Details about a Region little known.]

Mrs. Poynter's Missionary Box.
A Tale, by C. L. C., with an illustration. 18mo., paper cover, 2d.

[Shows how Indifference was roused to Action, and a Life rescued from discontent by the idea of Duty: for Parochial Use.]

My Two Years in an Indian Mission.
By the Rev. H. FIELD BLACKETT. Post 8vo., cloth boards, 1s. 6d.

[A fresh and graphic Account of Religious Work in India.]

Promadeni, a Biographical Sketch connected with the Indian Mission Among Women.
By EUGENIA VON MIZLAFF. 18mo., with three illustrations, cloth boards, 1s.

[A History of an Indian Conversion : for Young People.]

Sketches of our Life at Sarawak.
By HARRIETTE McDOUGALL. Crown 8vo., with map and four full-page illustrations. Cloth boards, 2s. 6d.

[Twenty years' experience of Mission Life in Sarawak. There is much interesting information concerning Rajah Brookes' Administration : for General Readers.]

Ten Years of Mission Life in British Guiana.
Being a Memoir of the Rev. Thomas Youd, by the Rev. W. T. VENESS. With map. Fcap. 8vo., limp cloth, 1s.

[An interesting account of Missionary Dangers and Incidents in this little known region : for General Use.]

The Missionary Church of England.
A Course of Six Sermons preached on the Afternoons of the Six Sundays after Easter, 1877, at St. James's, Westminster. Post 8vo., cloth boards, 1s. 4d.

[For intelligent Readers, &c.]

"Till the Day Break."
The Story of a Canadian Mission, by FREDERICK TRAVERS. Post 8vo, limp cloth, 6d.

[An interesting Tale of Mission Work.]

Under His Banner.
Papers on the Missionary Work of Modern Times. By the Rev. H. W. TUCKER, Secretary of the Society for the Propagation of the Gospel. Crown 8vo., with map, cloth boards, 5s.

[A Record of Missionary Labour, alike interesting to the Religious Man, the Patriot, and General Reader. Revised and brought up to date.]

THE HEATHEN WORLD AND ST. PAUL.

This Series is intended to throw Light upon the Writings and Labours of the Apostle of the Gentiles.

Fcap. 8vo., cloth boards, 2s. each.

St. Paul in Greece.
By the Rev. G. S. Davies. With Map.

St. Paul in Damascus and Arabia.
By the Rev. George Rawlinson, M.A., Canon of Canterbury. With Map.

St. Paul at Rome.
By the Very Rev. Charles Merivale, D.D., D.C.L., Dean of Ely. With Map.

St. Paul in Asia Minor and at the Syrian Antioch.
By the Rev. E. H. Plumptre, D.D. With Map.

ANCIENT HISTORY from the MONUMENTS.

This Series of Books is chiefly intended to illustrate the Sacred Scriptures by the results of recent Monumental Researches in the East.

Fcap. 8vo., cloth boards, 2s. each.

Assyria, from the Earliest Times to the Fall of Nineveh.
By the late George Smith, of the British Museum.

Sinai: from the Fourth Egyptian Dynasty to the Present Day.
By Henry S. Palmer, Major R. E., F.R.A.S. With Map.

Babylonia (The History of).
By the late George Smith. Edited by the Rev. A. H. Sayce.

Greek Cities and Islands of Asia Minor.
By the late W. S. W. Vaux, M.A.

Egypt from the Earliest Times to B.C. 300.
By the late S. Birch, LL.D.

Persia from the Earliest Period to the Arab Conquest.
By the late W. S. W. Vaux, M.A.

THE FATHERS FOR ENGLISH READERS.

A series of Monograms on the Chief Fathers of the Church, the Fathers selected being centres of influence at important periods of Church History and in important spheres of action.

Fcap. 8vo., cloth boards, 2s. each.

Leo the Great.
By the Rev. CHARLES GORE, M.A.

Gregory the Great.
By the Rev. J. BARMBY, B.D.

Saint Ambrose: his Life, Times, and Teaching.
By the Rev. ROBINSON THORNTON, D.D.

Saint Athanasius: his Life and Times.
By the Rev. R. WHELER BUSH. (2s. 6d.)

Saint Augustine.
By the Rev. E. L. CUTTS, B.A.

Saint Basil the Great.
By the Rev. RICHARD T. SMITH, B.D.

Saint Hilary of Poitiers, and Saint Martin of Tours.
By the Rev. J. GIBSON CAZENOVE, D.D.

Saint Jerome.
By the Rev. EDWARD L. CUTTS, B.A.

Saint John of Damascus.
By the Rev. J. H. LUPTON, M.A.

Synesius of Cyrene, Philosopher and Bishop.
By ALICE GARDNER.

The Apostolic Fathers.
By the Rev. H. S. HOLLAND.

The Defenders of the Faith; or, The Christian Apologists of the Second and Third Centuries.
By the Rev. F. WATSON, M.A.

The Venerable Bede.
By the Rev. G. F. BROWNE.

NON-CHRISTIAN RELIGIOUS SYSTEMS.

A Series of Manuals which furnish in a brief and popular form an accurate account of the great Non-Christian Religious Systems of the World.

Fcap. 8vo., cloth boards, 2s. 6d. each.

Buddhism: Being a Sketch of the Life and Teachings of Guatama, the Buddha.

By T. W. RHYS DAVIDS. With Map.

Buddhism in China.

By the Rev. S. BEAL. With Map.

Confucianism and Taouism.

By Professor ROBERT K. DOUGLAS, of the British Museum. With Map.

Hinduism.

By Professor MONIER WILLIAMS. With Map.

Islam and its Founder.

By J. W. H. STOBART. With Map.

Islam, as a Missionary Religion.

By CHARLES R. HAINES, M.A.

The Corân—Its Composition and Teaching, and the Testimony it bears to the Holy Scriptures.

By SIR WILLIAM MUIR, K.C.S.I.

LONDON:

NORTHUMBERLAND AVENUE, CHARING CROSS, W.C.;

43, QUEEN VICTORIA STREET, E.C.

BRIGHTON: 135, NORTH STREET.

.